Showdown at Dirt Crossing

When Hal Kramer rode into Dirt Crossing, he found that many things had changed – even the name of the place. But why had the saloon been closed down? And what was the secret of those tracks he had seen in the snow?

With the help of just one old-timer and his wife, Kramer prepares to take on local despot Zebulon King and his ruthless gang of hardcases. Hanging on the outcome are not only the lives of a group of outcasts taking refuge in the high mountains, but also the fate of the town itself.

As Kramer battles his way against overwhelming odds, one final question remains: will anyone stand by him when it comes to the final climactic showdown?

Showdown at Dirt Crossing

Jack Dakota

ROBERT HALE · LONDON

First published in Great Britain 2011

ISBN 978-0-7090-9154-7

Robert Hale Limited
Clerkenwell House
Clerkenwell Green
London EC1R 0HT

www.halebooks.com

Typeset by
Derek Doyle & Associates, Shaw Heath
Printed and bound in Great Britain by
CPI Antony Rowe, Chippenham and Eastbourne

CHAPTER ONE

Even before he hit town, Kramer knew that something was wrong. He had seen no one for a considerable time and there was no traffic along the broad trail that eventually would become the main street of town. Yet he had a certain feeling that he was being watched. Further back, before the snow had turned to sleet, he had detected traces of footprints. Getting down from his horse, he had examined the ground closely and concluded they were made by a little group of less than ten people. The strange thing was that there was no indication of horses. Drawing his field glasses from their case, he had scanned the surrounding country but had seen nothing. It was odd but it did not concern him. He had been travelling for a long time and was looking forward to a drink, a meal, soft sheets and a shave. He had money in his jeans and time on his hands. Whatever those tracks were about, it was none of his business.

He was riding an unusual mount, a piebald pinto

with notches cut into the tips of its ears; even without the evidence of the .50 Sharps rifle resting in its scabbard, the horse's markings would have indicated that its owner had at some stage earned his living as a buffalo hunter. He had been given it by a Kiowa chief and it was no cow horse. As he rode, his eyes flickered across the bottom lands and glanced from time to time towards the high hills and the distant mountains. A steady rain had turned into a damp low-lying mist but up there snow was falling and would be lying deep across the few trails. He had been following the course of a shallow stream which now took a turn. There was a narrow slatted wooden bridge but the horse seemed reluctant to cross over it so Kramer rode into the water and up the opposite bank to where the first outlying shacks and adobe buildings commenced. There was a wooden sign which looked new and read: *Kingsville: Population 959.* Kramer paused to examine it.

'Funny,' he said. 'Last time I passed this way the place was called Dirt Crossing.'

Over years of riding lonesome trails he had got into the habit of speaking out loud and addressing his horse.

'Seems a mite bigger too than I recall,' he added.

Touching his spurs to the horse's flanks, he rode on till he began to approach the centre of town. The main drag was wide and sticky with mud. It was unusually quiet; the few people who trod the boardwalks seemed to look at him with suspicion and even disapproval. He rode past the clapboard buildings, heading for the livery stables. He was also looking for the nearest saloon but there didn't seem to be one. The only building which still bore a saloon sign, the Golden Garter, was boarded up and deserted. There were other premises which might once have served that purpose but if so they were now given over to other enterprises – a bank, an insurance company, a clothing and outfitting emporium. Kramer looked in vain for somewhere where he might get a drink but the town was conspicuous by the absence of anything resembling a saloon or even a dance hall. Turning down a side street, he rode past more false-fronted shops and offices till he emerged on a small square. In one corner stood the marshal's office and jail-house and on the opposite side the livery stables. There was a small white-painted church from which issued the drone of people singing to a wheezy organ. *Odd,* Kramer reflected, *it ain't even Sunday.* Stopping outside the livery stables, he got down from his horse and led it up a ramp, calling for attention as he did so. After a few moments the figure of the ostler materialised through the gloom.

'Yeah?' he said in an inquiring tone.

'Strip him down,' Kramer said. 'Give him a good stall and extra oats and hay.'

The ostler looked Kramer up and down with a keen gaze which belied his bent back and grizzled features.

'Aimin' to stay long?' he asked.

'A few days. Maybe more.'

The ostler showed no interest in taking the pinto.

'Is there a decent hotel in town?' Kramer said.

The oldster thought for a moment before spitting into the dust.

'There's the Alhambra,' he said. 'Perhaps you'd better see about checkin' in first.'

'Why? Is there some sort of problem?'

The man shrugged.

'Don't get a lot of visitors,' he said, 'but I hear they got high standards.'

Kramer let out a low laugh.

'I'll take my chances,' he said.

The oldster seemed to consider his words.

'I got a better idea,' he said, 'if you'd be interested.'

'Yeah? What's that?'

'You could put up right here.'

Kramer glanced around.

'I ain't a horse,' he said.

The oldster's face relaxed into a grin, revealing a couple of worn, stained teeth.

'Nope,' he replied, 'I can see that.'

He chuckled.

'I got me a little place out back,' he said. 'Got a spare room with a real nice lookout. The old lady was lookin' to rent it out. She ain't been the same since Joshua left – that's our boy. Looked a bit like you – only younger, you understand. Rent's cheap and I can sure recommend her cookin'. Best steak pie this side of the Washita.'

Kramer was pensive.

'Seems kinda sudden,' he said. 'The offer I mean. You don't know me from Adam. You could be invitin' a heap of trouble into your household.'

'Maybe, but I don't think so. Besides, I ain't really got a lot of choice. As you can see, business is slack. We gotta find ways to survive.'

Kramer could see that there were only two horses in the stalls.

'It's up to you,' the ostler said. 'Why not freshen up and think about it? Come back and let me know.'

'I think I might do that, but is there somewhere I can get a drink first?' Kramer said.

The oldster rubbed his hand across his stubbled chin.

'Now there you got a problem,' he said. 'Fact of the matter is, all the saloons been closed up.'

He looked at Kramer with a twinkle in his eye.

'I got a bottle of Tanglefoot waitin' to be opened,' he said. 'Why don't we share a glass and I'll tell you the whole story.'

Kramer laughed again and then held out his hand.

'That's a real good offer,' he said. 'In fact, I think that settles matters. I reckon we got ourselves a deal.'

'Leave the hoss with me. Barber shop is on Main Street. See you back here when you're ready. The missus is sure goin' to enjoy makin' your acquaintance.'

Kramer stepped out into the street. Across the square the sounds of singing still drifted from the church. He paused for a moment to listen and then turned on to the main drag, looking for the barber shop. It was only a short distance away and there were no other customers. When he emerged, clean-shaven with his hair cut short and having enjoyed a hot bath, he felt reinvigorated. Looking across the drag, he saw further down the street what he was looking for, a building with the words *Down Home Eating House* scrawled in big green letters across the front. Even if he had to wait for something stronger to drink till he met up with the ostler, at least he could enjoy a hot black coffee. When he pushed open the door, it was to find the place deserted except for one customer who got up and left as he took a table by the window overlooking the street. The place looked neat and clean. There was a dresser containing crockery in one corner and a counter with a tidy looking young waitress standing behind it. She approached Kramer with a smile on her face.

'Just coffee,' Kramer said.

He was feeling quite hungry but in view of what the ostler had told him about his wife's cooking, he thought it might be better to wait in case he would be expected to eat with them. While he waited for the coffee he built a smoke and looked out of the window. Two men were lounging against a post on the opposite side of the street and something about their attitude aroused his interest. They were talking together but every now and then one or the other would look up and observe the restaurant. Maybe he was mistaken, but he had a notion that he was the object of their attention. The waitress returned with a pot of coffee and a tall mug.

'Any idea who those two are?' Kramer inquired, tilting his head in the direction of the men outside. Bending slightly to get a clearer view, the waitress nodded her head.

'Of course,' she said. 'That's Marshal Jack McLaren and his deputy Riff Rogers.'

'They seem to be interested in somethin' over here,' Kramer said.

'Probably just keepin' an eye on things. You're new in town aren't you?'

She moved away and, as if in response to the conversation Kramer had been having with her, one of the men began to cross the street. In a moment the door to the restaurant opened and the marshal appeared. He touched the brim of his hat to the waitress.

'Good morning, Miss Bird,' he said.

'Morning Marshal. Your usual?'

'Nothing for me at the moment.'

He turned to Kramer.

'Mind if I join you?'

The restaurant was empty and the request seemed odd. Nevertheless Kramer nodded in reply.

'Sure,' he said. 'Pull up a chair. Why not have a cup of coffee?'

He turned to the waitress.

'Could we have another cup?'

The marshal sat down opposite Kramer. He was tall and rather haggard looking and wore two guns despite the fact that the middle finger of his left hand was missing. The waitress returned with a cup and the marshal poured from the pot. When he had taken a drink he looked Kramer closely up and down.

'You're wearin' a side iron,' he said. 'That ain't allowed.'

Kramer unbuckled his gun belt.

'Take it,' he said. 'Didn't mean to cause no trouble. I'm new in town. Ain't familiar with the rules.'

He didn't mention the Sharps he had left behind with the ostler. The marshal took the gun belt and placed it on the table.

'Saw you ride in,' he said. 'That's a plumb strange kind of horse you're ridin', mister. Looked to me like an Indian paint.'

'No rule against that, I hope,' Kramer replied.

The marshal took another long sip of coffee.

'Aim to stay long?' he asked.

Kramer scratched the side of his head.

'A few days, maybe a week. Ain't sure yet. I'll see how it goes.'

'You checked in at the hotel?'

Kramer was about to tell the marshal about the ostler's offer but something about the marshal's attitude caused him to change his mind.

'Just on my way,' he said.

The marshal finished his drink and pushed aside his chair.

'We don't take too kindly to strangers,' he said. 'I'd recommend that you forget about that hotel room and just keep on ridin.'

'Is that some kind of warnin'?'

'Take it any way you please. If you want your guns back, call in at my office.'

Carrying the gun belt across his shoulder, he left the café. Kramer stubbed out the remains of his cigarette and turned to the waitress.

'What's bitin' him?' he asked. 'He sure don't seem too friendly.'

The waitress looked blankly in Kramer's direction.

'Maybe he's just having a bad day,' she said.

Rising to his feet, Kramer drew a bundle of dollar bills from his pocket and paid for the coffee. He pushed open the door of the restaurant and stepped out on to the boardwalk. There was no sign of the marshal but the man the waitress had referred to as his deputy was still standing on the other side of the street. As Kramer headed towards the livery stables he could feel the man's eyes on his back. He was more than ready for that drink.

Kramer had been right about the ostler's wife. When the door of the little house behind the stable was opened to his knock he smelt the delicious aroma of cooking.

'Figured you might be needin' some chow,' the ostler said. 'Come right in. Let me introduce you to the wife.'

At that moment an inner door opened and a woman emerged with a tea-towel in her hand. She had grey hair tied behind in a bun and her small frame seemed inadequate to support the weight of her enormous breasts.

'Hello,' she said. 'My husband has been tellin' me about you.'

The ostler turned to Kramer.

'Don't believe we've introduced ourselves. I'm Bruford, Jess Bruford – guess you maybe saw the name over the door of the livery, and this is Clara.'

'Hal Kramer. Real pleased to make your acquaintance.'

There was a gurgling sound from the kitchen.

'You'll have to excuse me,' Clara said, 'I got things just comin' to the boil.' She turned and scuttled from the room.

'Liver and bacon,' Bruford commented. 'Here, come with me and I'll show you the room.'

Kramer followed the old man up some stairs. Two doors led off the landing.

'Big one's ours,' Bruford commented. 'This other one is yours.'

He opened the door and stepped to one side for Kramer to enter. The room was as the oldster had just described it, small and sparsely furnished. There was a bed and a chest of drawers with a pitcher of water standing on it. A small mirror hung on the wall together with a daguerreotype of a young man who looked sheepishly out at the viewer.

'My son, Jordan,' the oldster commented, seeing Kramer's attention had been fixed on it. 'Used to be his room. Not likely to need it again. He's gone east. Doin' well.'

Kramer's eyes strayed to the window which gave a view on to a small back lawn and a narrow lane with a few other houses. Peering over the rooftops was the thin steeple of the church.

'This'll do me fine,' Kramer said, 'as long as you're still sure about havin' me. Like I said, I wasn't aimin' to stay too long anyways, but it seems like it might be less than I thought.'

The oldster looked at him questioningly and then a grin spread across his countenance.

'Don't tell me,' he said. 'Marshal McLaren got to you already?'

Kramer nodded.

'He didn't exactly give me a warm welcome.'

Any further conversation on the matter was interrupted by the voice of Clara Bruford calling up the stairs that dinner was ready.

'Comin' right down,' Jess called back, and turning aside to Kramer, added:

'We'll have a word or two later. I haven't forgotten about that Tanglefoot.'

Clara Bruford's cooking proved to be just as good as the oldster had promised. By the time Kramer had put away his second helping of apple pie he couldn't have eaten another bite.

'Let me help with the washing,' he volunteered but the old lady would have none of it.

'Just you two relax. Sit out on the veranda. I'll join you when I'm finished.'

Kramer stepped outside. The air was damp but the wind had switched directions and it wasn't cold. He sat down on a cane chair and in a few moments he was joined by Bruford carrying a bottle and three glasses. He poured two stiff drinks and then collapsed into a chair next to his guest.

'Guess you've been waitin' for this,' he said.

'Sure have.'

Kramer tipped his head and swallowed a mouthful. The next second he was blowing hard and struggling to resist the urge to cough. The liquor burned its way down his throat but when it had gone down it felt warm and glowing in his stomach.

'Hell,' he stuttered. 'That sure hits the spot.'

The oldster's glass was already empty. He had obviously developed a resistance over time.

'Thought you might appreciate it,' he replied.

Kramer took another sip and then looked out over the lawn to the church spire. Bats were circling near a stand of trees and from somewhere an owl hooted.

'Tell me about the marshal,' he said.

Bruford gave a grunting sound.

'Yeah,' he replied. 'I reckon there's a few things you maybe ought to know about Kingsville.'

'Didn't it used to be Dirt Crossing?'

The oldster looked surprised.

'You been this way before?' he said.

'Once, a long time ago. I bin around. Wasn't stayin', just passin' through.'

'As far as I'm concerned, it's still Dirt Crossing. Was that way until about two years ago. That's about when Zebulon King became mayor. He'd been a big noise about town for a long time before that, but after he became mayor it just went to his head. Now the whole place pretty well belongs to him. He appointed McLaren as marshal and he does whatever King tells him to. King doesn't let anyone stand in his way. If he even suspects that people might not agree with him, he takes measures to deal with them.'

'What? He eliminates them?'

'Oh, nothin' quite so obvious as that, although I reckon he's just about capable of anythin'. That's why you won't find any saloons in town. Just lately King took it into his head to embark on some kind of moral crusade. He was clever enough to get most of the townsfolk on his side with talk of moral degeneracy and the threat to decent behaviour from certain elements. Then he ordered all the saloons to close, rounded up a few token scapegoats and had them driven outa town.'

Suddenly Kramer remembered those traces of footprints he had found.

'Let me guess,' he said. 'About seven or eight folk would it be?'

'How did you know? But you're right. There'd be maybe that number, all pretty insignificant figures so that no one really cared while at the same time they'd act as a warnin' to anyone else.'

'What sort of figures?'

'A few saloon girls, what you might call the soiled doves of Dirt Crossing, a couple of bums, one or two hangers-on at the gamblin' tables: you can guess the types.'

'And he just ran 'em out of town without even any horses?'

Again the oldster looked at Kramer with a puzzled expression.

'Heck, for a stranger you seem to know quite a bit.'

'I seen their sign,' Kramer responded. 'There weren't no trace of horses.'

'Some folks objected but King had done his homework. He made sure he had the backing of the town council. He worked on the members, and as a last resort he always has the marshal to back him up.'

'You were one of the objectors?'

'Sure, I raised my voice but it weren't no good.'

Kramer finished his drink and the ostler sat forward to pour him another.

'And that's one reason why you were lookin' for a lodger, even if it was only for a few days.'

The oldster looked uneasy.

'Sorry,' Kramer added. 'But you said yourself business wasn't too good. I saw you only got two horses in the stalls.'

'Yeah, I guess you're right. But that weren't the only reason.'

Just then the door to the house opened and Clara Bruford stepped on to the veranda. She took a seat beside Kramer and her husband poured a good measure of whiskey into the third glass. She lifted it and took a good long swallow.

'What's he been sayin' to you?' she said to Kramer.

'I bin tellin' him a little bit about what's been happenin' lately in Dirt Crossing,' Jess replied. 'He's already met the marshal.'

'Lordy, he don't want to hear all our troubles,' she replied, and turning to Kramer, added:

'Just make yourself comfortable and don't pay no heed. Things ain't necessarily as bad as he likes to make out.'

'What? You're goin' to say that at least things is peaceable,' Bruford responded. 'Maybe you got a point, but things weren't so bad even before King took over. But even so, havin' him and his cronies decidin' what's allowed and what ain't allowed is too big a price to pay. Some day someone is goin' to have to take a stand against him. Isn't bein' free what this country's all about?'

Kramer took a swallow of the whiskey. He was getting used to it now.

'I'm interested,' he said. 'Besides, I got a stake in things now.'

'Yeah?' Bruford responded. 'How's that?'

'If it weren't for you, where would I have got a drink?'

Bruford grinned and his wife laughed. For a while there was silence before Kramer spoke again.

'Weather's been bad recently,' he said.

'Yes, this is about the first half decent night we've had,' Clara replied.

She turned to look at Kramer.

'I guess you're thinkin' the same as us,' she said, including her husband in her comments.

'Yeah. There's some pretty sorry folks somewhere out there,' he said. 'Folks who will be findin' it real hard to survive. I reckon somethin' needs to be done.'

'That's what we were figurin',' Bruford replied.

'First thing in the mornin' I'm goin' to ride out, see if I can find 'em. See what sort of state they're in.'

'And I'm comin' with you,' Bruford replied.

His wife got to her feet.

'I'm glad that's decided,' she said. 'Right now you'll have to excuse me. I'm gettin' kinda tired and you boys will need a good feedin' before you set out.'

She made her way back into the house. Bruford lifted the bottle and held it in the light from the window.

'Not much left,' he said. 'Would be a pity to leave it.'

He poured the rest of it into their two glasses.

'Still, I got plenty more where that come from,' he said.

Some days earlier the little party of outcasts of whom Jess Bruford had been speaking stood in a little huddled bunch and watched the buckboard which had carried them out of town as it made its way back to Kingsville. They had been given little warning and had nothing much apart from the clothes on their backs. There were seven of them, four women and three men. Three of the women were young and underneath their coats were still dressed in the fineries they wore to attract customers in the saloon. The other woman was similarly attired but she was older and, gathering the others about her, seemed to adopt a proprietary and almost motherly role. It suited her. She was large and handsome and her blonde hair was gathered in a high pompadour.

'No good coyotes,' she said, addressing the man standing next to her.

The other two men were middle-aged, down at heel and nondescript, but this man was different. Tall and slim, he wore a long black jacket with matching trousers, a fancy dark red waistcoat and a white shirt and string tie. In his hand he held a wide brimmed soft hat to reveal long black hair which was slicked back and almost reached his shoulders at the back.

'Your description is accurate,' he replied, 'although it may be somewhat disrespectful to the coyote breed.'

One of the girls started to cry. The sky was overcast and already they were beginning to feel the chill.

'No point in standing here,' the man said. 'It's my

opinion that the first requirement is to find some kind of shelter. I believe we are most of us acquainted with one another?'

Some of the others nodded.

'In case anyone does not know me, my name is Armitage, Reynard Armitage.'

He turned to the older lady.

'Of course, Miss Tilly and I have known each other for some time, although I never did quite get your patronymic.'

'I ain't too sure what you mean,' she replied.

'Forgive me. I meant your surname, madam.'

'Oh, in that case it's Lush. Great balls of fire, I haven't used that in a long time. Everyone just calls me Tilly.'

When the introductions were over, Armitage pointed to a large bundle which was lying on the ground.

'They appear not to have left us much in the way of sustenance,' he said. 'I guess that will be our second problem.'

One of the other men spat and turned an unshaved face towards him.

'Hell,' he said, 'they ain't even left us a gun to protect ourselves.'

'Well, my friend, that's just where you're wrong,' Armitage replied.

Reaching into his waistcoat, he produced a double-barrelled .41 calibre rim-fire pistol that had been concealed in a shoulder holster.

'I would have preferred something more substantial,' he said, 'but it's better than nothin'.'

Tilly Lush regarded him with a smile on her face.

'You're very resourceful, Mr Armitage,' she said.

Armitage acknowledged her compliment with a nod and a smile before putting his hat back on his head.

'I think we had better start walking,' he said. 'I'm afraid, however, that I am not familiar with the country. Would any of you have any suggestions as to which direction we should take? Obviously not towards town.'

The man who had commented on their lack of weapons spoke again.

'I did some trappin' up in these hills,' he said. 'It was a long time ago. There was a little shack. Maybe it's still there.'

'Do you think you could find your way to it?'

The man looked about him thoughtfully. They had been deposited in the foothills and the mountains stood frowning back of them.

'I just ain't too sure. I guess if we head further up into the peaks we'll be on the right track.'

'Lead on, my friend. After all, we haven't got a real lot of choice.'

Bending down, Armitage picked up the bundle of provisions and they started up the track. At first the going was quite easy but after a time the path got steeper. A cold wind had sprung up and came blowing at them from the snow-capped mountains.

The ground was muddy and caught at their feet and after a time a light rain began to fall. The three girls were shivering and moaning. Apart from the man who was leading the way, whose name was Bentner, the others were silent and surly. One of them began to cough and every so often the party had to halt to let him catch his breath. They were climbing through an area of grass with rocky outcrops but not far ahead of them the trees began, mainly ponderosa pine and fir. What traces of a trail into the mountains they had been following seemed to have vanished.

'You sure you know the way?' Armitage said, walking alongside the older man.

'Like I said, it was a long time ago. One place looks pretty much like another.'

Armitage had his doubts about the man's credentials but kept his counsel to himself. He didn't want to upset the girls more than they were already. They had been climbing for some time and it seemed to him necessary that they find somewhere to make camp soon. His eyes scanned the terrain, looking for anything that might offer some chance of respite from the rain, which was now whipping up stronger in the gathering wind. Off to his right the land dropped away into a small basin with a stand of aspen. It wasn't much, but it offered something better than the naked slopes they had been climbing. The others had stopped again and he made his way to investigate more closely. At the bottom of the basin there were some boulders among the trees and there was a sound of trickling water. He returned to the others.

'It'll be getting dark real soon,' he said. 'I would suggest we make our way to the hollow and endeavour to make ourselves as comfortable as we might.'

There was no opposition. Following him, they made their way to the basin and dropped down beneath its sheltering walls. While the others sank exhausted to the ground, he looked about for bark and leaves to make a fire and found some relatively dry branches which might serve the purpose. Returning to the others, he eventually got a fire going.

'Well,' he said, 'I imagine that we're about ready to make a repast. Let's see what the good marshal has provided for us.'

He bent down and opened the bundle. There was some bacon, a supply of beans, strips of jerky, bread and biscuits and a stock of coffee. There were also some basic cooking utensils.

'Come on, girls,' Miss Tilly said, 'You can help me. Let's see what we can do.'

Armitage smiled at her. He realized she was doing her best to keep the three girls from dwelling too much on their dire plight. With her encouragement they set about rustling up a semblance of a meal. Armitage was content to sit and watch. In the shelter of the rocks and under a canopy of leaves, their situation for the moment was quite passable. In addition, the rain seemed to have died away and they were sheltered by the banks of the basin from the worst of the wind. He listened to it whining in the trees. He hadn't noticed that Bentner was absent and sat up when he heard footsteps. The man was returning with water from the stream and soon they had a pot of coffee boiling on the flames. There were only two tin cups but that was OK. By the time they had bacon and beans and some strong black coffee in their stomachs they were all feeling a little better. The fire was warm and its glow was comforting. Every now and again Armitage threw some branches into the flames. Nobody spoke much. The girls were soon asleep. One of the men produced a pack of Bull Durham and they built smokes, Miss Tilly included. Armitage felt in his pocket where he kept a flask of whiskey. He was tempted to offer it round but desisted. It might be needed later. Finally he and Miss Tilly were the only ones awake. Their eyes met across the flickering firelight and there was a recognition in them that if they were to have any chance of survival, it was down to them. Armitage began to think about what might be in store but presently his eyes closed and the last image he carried into sleep was the figure of the saloon proprietress as she adjusted a coat over the recumbent form of one of her girls.

CHAPTER TWO

Kramer opened his eyes. It was still dark but already he could hear sounds of movement and activity outside. Going to the window, he looked down into the yard. A wagon was drawn up and two indistinct figures in whom he recognized the Brufords were moving about loading boxes into it. Putting on his shirt and trousers, he clattered down the stairs.

' 'Mornin',' he said. 'What's goin' on?'

Clara came up to him.

'Go back inside,' she said. 'It's a mite cold out here. Just give me a few minutes and I'll see about rustlin' up some breakfast.'

'Don't worry about that,' he replied. 'Let me give you a hand with whatever you're busy with.'

Jess Bruford came staggering by with a large carton.

'Sleep OK?' he enquired.

'Here, let me take that. You shoulda woke me up sooner.'

'Figure those folks will be needin' supplies,' the oldster said. 'If'n we ever find 'em, that is.'

Kramer hadn't thought about it. He had merely assumed they would ride out in search of the exiles. Now he saw the sense of what the Brufords were doing. By the time the first rays of sunlight were brightening the eastern horizon, they had finished packing the wagon and were seated at table enjoying a hearty breakfast.

'Me and the old girl been thinkin',' Jess commented. 'Maybe it'd be a better idea if me an' her come along with the wagon while you ride on ahead and try to find where those folks are.'

Kramer considered the proposition.

'It was my idea,' Clara said. 'Really, I don't want to be left behind.'

'It makes sense whatever way you look at it,' Jess said. 'This contraption ain't goin' to be puttin' on any head of steam. You'll be able to travel faster and have a much better chance of discoverin' any sign if you can move on your own.'

The idea made sense to Kramer too.

'We'll keep in contact,' he said. 'I'll ride back to let you know if I find anythin'. Have you got a gun?'

The oldster grinned.

'Naturally,' he replied. 'Got a couple of Army Colts for you too. Didn't you say the marshal had acquired your own artillery?'

'That's great,' Kramer said. 'If you get into any trouble, fire a couple of shots.'

'What sort of trouble are we likely to run in to?' Clara said, looking up from loading another pile of bacon and beans on to their plates.

Kramer looked blank and then shrugged.

'I don't know,' he said. 'But I'd say there was already a heap of trouble brewin' if what you've told me is correct.' The old lady paused and then laughed. 'Yep,' she said. 'I surely see what you mean.' She turned to her husband.

'Heck, Jess,' she said, 'I ain't been so excited since we fought off the Hoover boys. I'm beginnin' to enjoy myself.'

The old man grinned back at her.

'More coffee would sure be appreciated,' he said. He turned to Kramer.

'What if you're too far off to hear any gunshots?'

'Then you've to get Clara to handle things,' Kramer replied.

It was still dark when the wagon rolled out of the rear of the livery stable. Sitting high were the Brufords and riding alongside was Kramer on the pinto, leading a pack-horse. They travelled a little way down a back street which led past some warehouses and abandoned barns before eventually emerging on to the trail which led to the little bridge over the shallow stream. The wagon rattled across while Kramer waded the horses through the water.

'That's goin' to have to change some day,' Bruford shouted, pointing at the sign.

'Sure is,' Kramer responded. 'This place is goin'

back to bein' Dirt Crossing.'

'Might not be that easy,' Clara muttered.

Kramer continued to ride alongside the wagon for another couple of miles and then rode his horse up close.

'I'll be leavin' you folks at this point,' he said. 'Remember what we said.'

'Please, do your best to locate those poor people,' Clara replied. 'They may not have been ideal citizens, but they didn't deserve this.'

'Don't worry, I'll be doin' just that. I'll find 'em.'

'Which way do you reckon they would have headed?'

'Towards the mountains. Carry on down this track and then turn generally in that direction. Be seein' you folks.'

Without waiting for a reply, Kramer dug in his spurs and started off at a quicker pace down the trail. The horse responded and stretched out its legs. When Kramer glanced back, the wagon was already a long way behind.

He had no special reason for suggesting the mountains as the direction in which to seek the missing group other than it would be where he would have headed. There was a better chance of finding shelter up there and a better prospect of putting up resistance in case of attack from any quarter. Besides, from what he had been able to glean from the traces of footprints he had discovered, they were moving towards the hills. His first instinct had been to try and find that spot but then he figured there would be no point; any further traces of their passage would have been obliterated by now. It seemed a better idea to press ahead towards the peaks and see what he might pick up there. The wind had gathered and he pulled his coat collar up and his hat brim down. It was very cold and, thinking of the little group of outcasts, he began to feel sorry for them. What kind of a man was this King? What sort of a person would abandon helpless folks to their fate in this weather, with little or nothing to sustain them? If he was as big as Bruford had indicated, what had he to fear from a bunch of outsiders anyway? But that was probably just the point. King had most likely got to his position of eminence by just such intimidating behaviour. After he had located the refugees it might be time to pay King a call. He realized how little he knew about the man. When this immediate business was settled, he would have to talk further with the old timer.

After a time he slowed his horse down to its customary pace. It was lean and rangy and covered the miles easily. He was in the foothills now and climbing steadily. Above him reared the high snow-capped peaks, at present wreathed in lowering clouds. Suddenly he stopped and jumped from the saddle. On the ground there were unmistakable indications of a wagon having passed that way some time before. Again Kramer got to thinking of the man behind this act of eviction. He had made pretty certain of dropping his victims far from the town and in an isolated spot. He might as well have killed them outright because there was little chance they could survive for long. Looking very carefully, he found traces of their passage. Some of the grass still bore the imprint of feet. Some of the longer strands remained bent in one direction.

Leading the horses, he continued a little further but soon had to admit defeat. The ground was getting rockier and it was too difficult to read the sign any further. An Indian would have done it easily; he wished he had his old Kiowa friend with him. As it was, he mounted the pinto and continued to ride, the horse now stepping nimbly across the rock-strewn hillside, with the pack-horse bringing up the rear. He went on for what seemed a long time. Looking about him, he thought he detected sign of deer. If a man knew the mountain country he would be able to live off it. But it was unlikely any of the group he was searching for would be able to do so even if they had weapons. It was unlikely any of them would survive for long and conditions were getting bleaker by the hour. The clouds were gathering and dropping lower, draping themselves over the mountains like a shroud. The wind was blowing harder and whistling across the exposed surfaces. The only other sounds were the occasional snicker of his horse, the creak of saddle leather and the muffled beat of hoofs on the sparse grass. Kramer glanced behind to make sure the pack-horse was OK, and then he thought he heard another sound. It was very faint and at first he ignored it but then it came again, a faint moaning which mingled with the soughing of the wind. He brought the pinto to a halt. Straining his ears, he listened for a repetition of the sound but nothing came. Eventually he concluded that he must be mistaken and was about to ride on when he heard it again. This time he knew what it was – the low plaint of someone in distress. Ahead of him there was a patch of vegetation and the sound seemed to come from that direction. Urging his horse forward, he rode into the bushes, emerging into a little clearing in the middle of them. Beside a rock lay the prostrate figure of a young woman. She was wearing a yellow satin dress over which were draped a couple of coats which offered but little protection from the elements. Kramer muttered something beneath his breath and then slid from the saddle. In another second he was kneeling by her side.

'Just hold on, lady,' he said.

She looked up at him with dazed eyes.

'Are you hurt?'

There was no response so he quickly got to his feet and went to his horse. Reaching into his saddlebags, he came back with a blanket and a slicker. He also had a flask of water.

'Take a little bit,' he said.

Lifting her head gently, he held the flask to her mouth. She opened her lips and a few drops trickled down her throat. It wasn't much but it seemed to do her some good. She looked at him again and this time her eyes were more focused. Making a big effort, she tried to sit upright but immediately slumped back again.

'Don't try anythin' just yet,' Kramer said.

The woman's clothes were wet and she was shivering. Covering her with the blanket and the slicker, Kramer began to gather together some branches and leaves to make a fire. Working as quickly as he could, it didn't take too long till he had a fire going. He threw more sticks on to it and soon the place was suffused with a warm glow. He put a pot of water to boil on the flames and made coffee. When he had finished he turned back to the woman. She was still lying flat but when he sat down beside her she succeeded in raising herself on one elbow.

'Whoever you are,' she said, 'I thank you.'

'Are you feelin' a little better?' he asked.

She gave a nod.

'My name's Kramer,' he said. 'Hal Kramer. I would take a guess that you are one of the people got run out of town.'

The shadow of a frown appeared on her brow.

'My foot,' she said. 'I hurt my foot. I couldn't walk. The others said they'd come back for me.'

'When was that?' Kramer said.

She shook her head. 'I don't know. I must have passed out and slept.'

'Is your foot hurting now? Which one is it?'

'It's the left one. It seems a bit better at the moment.'

'Maybe I'd better take a look.'

Her face puckered as very carefully Kramer untied her shoe.

'Tell me if it hurts,' he said.

She nodded but said nothing. Kramer couldn't help but notice the look of pain on her face and her clenched teeth. When he had managed to take off her shoe he could see that the foot was swollen and bruised. It must have been painful but she had not flinched or let out a sound. She was a game one. Kramer did what he could to bandage the swelling, using his bandanna, and then he went back to where the horses were tethered, returning with a slim silver flask. It contained whiskey and he poured a little into a mug of hot black coffee.

'Here,' he said, 'drink this. It might help.'

She took a mouthful, grimacing slightly, but it seemed to work.

'I haven't told you my name,' she said. 'It's Bonny, Bonny Lange.'

'Real nice to meet you,' he said and, now that he had a chance to look at her more closely, he meant it.

'How did you find me?' she said.

In a few words Kramer explained his presence on the hillside.

'What happened to you?' he concluded.

'There were eight of us. We were looking for a

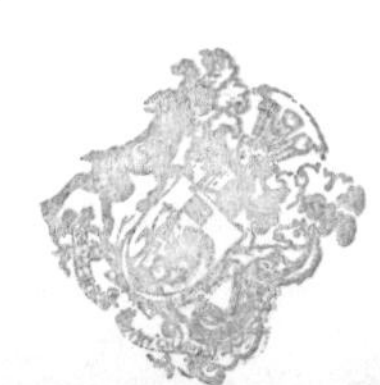

cabin one of the others knew about. I slipped and twisted my ankle. They didn't know what to do. One of the men said they couldn't wait, they needed to find the cabin. There was an argument between him and another man, I think his name is Armitage. I've seen him in the saloon; he's a gambler. Armitage carried me a little way but then he had to give up. He made me as comfortable as he could and said he'd be back to get me. He and Miss Lush, that's the woman who runs the Golden Garter, didn't want to leave me behind but I think they had no choice.'

Kramer was silent, weighing up the situation.

'We'll stay here for now,' he said. 'I reckon a storm is brewin' and this is as good a spot as we're likely to find. Guess you must be hungry?'

'I wasn't till now,' she replied.

'Make yourself as comfortable as you can. I'll rustle us up somethin' to eat.'

Kramer suited his actions to his words and soon they were eating strips of bacon with beans. Between the rock and the bushes they were fairly well protected when the storm finally burst, making the fire crackle as drops of rain slipped though the barrier of branches and leaves Kramer had rigged up to augment what was already there. By the time she had finished eating the girl seemed a lot happier and her clothes had dried in the heat of the fire. Kramer had got other blankets to cover her with from the packhorse, leaving himself nothing but the sheepskin jacket he wore.

'You'd best get some sleep,' he said. 'Night will be coming on soon. We'll need to move early in the morning.'

She didn't remonstrate as the ordeal through which she had passed began to exert its effect. Closing her eyes, she dozed away for a while before waking again with a shudder.

'You must be cold,' she said, looking across to where Kramer crouched by the dwindling fire.

'I'll be fine,' he replied. He picked up a few more branches and threw them on the flames.

'It seems a mite silly for me to be snug and warm under these blankets and you out there with nothing but the clothes you're wearin',' she said.

'Like I say, I'll be fine.'

'There's plenty of room under here for us both,' she replied.

Kramer hesitated. Normally he would have known how to take such an offer, but there was something about this girl that was different, despite her saloon girl's attire. He felt she was making the offer at face value. Besides, she was in no condition to be considering anything else and he was certainly feeling the cold. Like she said, it made sense. Getting to his feet, he walked over to where she lay and then slid down beside her under the blankets. He placed his guns where he could reach them and then turned to thank her but she was already asleep.

Kramer awoke with a start in the middle of the night to find snow falling heavily. Already it had drifted over them and the fire had long been extinguished. A cold wind was blowing down the mountain and somewhere a wolf howled. Taking care not to awaken the sleeping girl, he crawled out of the blankets and started to gather branches and dead wood to rebuild the fire. Nearby the horses shifted their feet and when he had a fire going he moved them in closer and fed them come corn. He put a pot of coffee to heat over the flames and when it was ready he shook the girl gently to awaken her. For a moment there was a frightened look in her eyes and then, as her senses returned and she perceived who it was, she relaxed and smiled.

'Sorry to wake you up,' he said, 'but I reckon we'd best be movin'.'

Sitting up, she rubbed the sleep from her eyes.

'Is it morning?' she asked.

'Soon will be.'

'It's snowing,' she said inconsequentially.

He poured a cup of coffee and held it to her lips.

'Here, drink this.'

They sat together in silence while the fire gathered in strength and kept the cold at bay. Presently she looked at him.

'Where are we goin' to move to?' she asked.

Strangely, the question took him by surprise. He had taken for granted that they would go back to town. He had forgotten that she was outlawed. He began to think about the matter. Maybe they could sneak back without being observed, but from what he had gathered about King's hold on the place they might have problems. Having despatched the unfortunate outcasts, King would be certain to take steps to make sure that none of them ever came back, or if they tried to, that he would at least know about it. Besides, it would be unfair to expect the Brufords to take the risk of concealing her. They would do it all right, he knew that, but he didn't want to impose on them. In any case, he wasn't sure where they were now. Presumably they were camped somewhere with the wagon. That was their best chance. Turning his attention to the girl, he explained about the Brufords.

'That was real good of them to come out lookin' for us,' she said. 'They sound like real nice people.'

'They are nice people,' he replied, 'and they shouldn't be too hard to find.'

For a little longer they enjoyed the warmth of the fire and then as it died down again Kramer got to his feet and began to saddle up. The pinto showed some restlessness but he calmed it down with a few whispered words.

'Will the horses be OK on the mountain?'

'They'll be fine,' Kramer said.

He had reservations about riding out in the night but there was little choice. Stay much longer and they would get colder and colder and more and more depleted while the conditions got worse. Looking about, he could detect a lightening of the darkness which presaged the approach of dawn.

'OK, ready?' he asked.

The girl nodded her head. Bending down, Kramer picked her up and, carrying her to his horse, hoisted her on to its back. She flinched a little and couldn't help a muted groan escaping from her lips but otherwise she offered no resistance. Kramer couldn't help but notice how light and frail she felt in his arms. Getting up behind her, he touched his spurs to the horse's flanks and it began to pick its way down the mountainside, walking with a delicate tread, wary of the snow, the pack-horse trailing along behind. Kramer had considered letting her ride it, but had decided against it. Later, perhaps, when she was stronger and her foot was better, but for the moment he felt she needed his presence and support. The world around them was suffused with a luminous transparency although the high peaks were hidden by dark, dense clouds. The snow relented for a short time and then began to fall with renewed vigour. Slowly and carefully the pinto stepped while Kramer examined the terrain for possible hazards. In hollows on either side of the trail the snow had gathered in deepening drifts and he was anxious that the horses should avoid them. Even so at one point the pinto stepped off into deep snow and began to flounder, dragging the pack-horse with it. Kramer reined in hard and the plunging pinto fought its way back to firmer ground.

'Good boy,' Kramer called, and then, putting his mouth close to Bonny's ear, he said:

'That's why I wanted to start early. Give it a bit longer and the trail could become impassable.'

She was silent for a moment before replying.

'I wonder what's become of the others? They won't last long in weather like this.'

Kramer said nothing. She was right: he didn't give much for their chances either but there was no point in saying so. Once they had found the Bruford wagon and he had left her in their care, he would do what he could to continue the search and find them. But already it could be too late.

Daylight struggled to arrive. The sky was black and the snowstorm raged without abate. It was difficult for Kramer to see very far ahead and the deepening snow made it impossible for him to detect any sign. The wagon might have got this far up the mountain and passed right by where they were riding but any tracks would have been completely obliterated. They had been riding for a considerable time and he was tempted to stop but decided to keep pushing on. Although they had come down from the higher ground the way was still difficult and the horses made but a plodding progress. His eyes were being dazzled by the snow so it was with some shock that he suddenly saw the wagon looming up ahead of them. It was difficult to perceive with its white canvas covering and they were almost upon it before they realized it was there. It wasn't where Kramer would have expected to find it and it was leaning at an odd angle with its wheels deep in the snow. There were no horses. Kramer brought the pinto to a halt and leaped from the saddle.

'Quick,' he said, stretching up his arms, 'Come down and wait behind that rock.'

Indicating the one he meant, he lifted her down and carried her over to it.

'Keep your head low,' he said, 'I'll be back in a moment.'

'Is there something wrong?' she asked.

'Just do as I tell you,' he said.

Walking toward the wagon, his legs sinking in snow half way to his knees, he felt a nauseous sense of dread clawing at his stomach. He had not heard any gunshots but he feared what he might find. Drawing his six-gun, he came to the back of the wagon and holding back the canvas, peered inside. Blood was spattered up the sides of the wagon and a pool of it lay congealing on the floor. Lying together with their arms outstretched and empty eyes staring at the roof of the wagon were two bodies. Kramer's stomach contracted to a hard knot and then suddenly seemed to expand again. Looking closely, he could see that the bodies were not those of Jess Bruford and his wife, but two others. Quickly he moved round to the front of the wagon. The horses had been removed from their traces but the snow-covered ground yielded no clues as to what had occurred. Kramer kneeled down and began to fumble in the snow. Eventually his fingers discovered an empty cartridge case. There must be others but the one he had found was enough. It was obvious that the Brufords had been attacked. They must have fought back, but what had been the outcome? Whoever their attackers were, they must have prevailed otherwise the horses would not be gone. In which case, how to account for the two corpses in the wagon? Turning, Kramer went back to the wagon and climbed inside. The stores and supplies were still there where they had been loaded, more or less untouched. The attackers had not been interested in them. Kramer was still trying to account for what had happened when he suddenly remembered the girl; he had been so pre-occupied that he had temporarily forgotten her. Jumping down, he returned to where he had left her behind the rock. She was still just as he had left her and showed no further signs of anxiety. He realized that he had been so concerned about what might have happened to his friends that all sense of time had vanished. He seemed to have been away too long; in fact it had only been a matter of few minutes since he had left her.

'Are your friends there?' she breathed.

Her teeth were chattering and she couldn't help shivering with the cold. Briefly he explained what he had found.

'Give me another minute or two,' he said. 'I'll just sort things out in the wagon and then perhaps you could move inside.'

When he returned he threw the corpses overboard, not bothering to check to see who they might be. He had a pretty good idea that they were King's men. Working quickly, he covered them over with snow and then cleaned up the wagon as best he could. It didn't take long to remove the worst of the stains and to have the wagon looking almost respectable. Once he had finished he collected the girl and installed her in the wagon. It wasn't much but it offered protection from the snow and it was certainly less cold inside than it was out. Then he hitched the horses to the wagon. He was glad now that he had the extra horse. It had proven to be a reliable animal, a roan gelding, and with the two horses pulling together, he felt more confident that they would be able to extricate the wagon and move onwards. When the horses were in the traces, he grabbed a spade from the wagon and jumping down, began to shovel snow from around the wheels and from the path ahead. Then he climbed to the wagon seat and pulled on the reins, encouraging the horses with shouts. The wagon lurched forward and then settled back into the snow. Cursing under his breath, he got back down to take another look at the wagon wheels. The rear wheels were on firmer ground. Getting back up, he began to unload the wagon of some of its heavier items in order to make it lighter. Then he blocked the rear wheels, unhooked the traces and led one of the horses to the back of the wagon. Fastening a rope to each side of the axle underneath, he slapped the horse across the rump, tugging on the reins and encouraging it to pull.

Slowly at first but then with a jolt the front wheels came up out of the snow. Re-rigging the horses, he loaded the wagon as quickly as he could and climbed back on the seat. He backed up the wagon, taking care to avoid the worst of the snow, and then hauled on the reins. This time the wheels held the track and the wagon lumbered forward. Turning his head, he called back into the wagon:

'You OK, Miss Lange?'

There was no reply. Turning right round, he peered inside. He had laid the girl on a blanket on the floor and covered her with other blankets. Now she was fast asleep.

'Best thing for her,' he muttered to himself.

He fell back to wondering what had become of the Brufords. He couldn't work it out to his entire satisfaction, but it seemed to him that the likeliest scenario was that the Brufords had either fought off an initial attack and then abandoned the wagon, or seen the assailants coming and done the same. The attackers had taken the horses. Two of them had come back and had been caught unawares by the Brufords' return. Those were the two whose corpses he had found in the wagon. He smiled grimly to himself at the thought; that oldster sure had some grit about him. They had then taken the men's horses and ridden away, presumably taking some provisions with them but abandoning the rest. It seemed to fit the facts and he only hoped he was correct because if he was, it meant his friends were still alive. But where were they and how were they coping? They might be a pair of tough old goats, but they were oldsters nonetheless. There was no point in speculating further. He had plenty of immediate problems to deal with and he was no nearer finding the rest of the refugees. He simply had two more to add to the list.

For what seemed a considerable length of time Kramer drove the wagon back down the mountain-side. He had no definite idea as to where he was heading but it made sense for the present to get down from the high ground. Snow continued to fall but gradually faded to a steady insistent unloading of the leaden skies. The horses picked their own way and as the wagon gently swayed from side to side, he began to feel sleepy. His eyes closed and then opened again, closed and opened. They were about to close once more when suddenly they detected something on the hillside above. Kramer didn't know what it was, but the next instant a crump of air and the booming echo of rifle fire told him he was not mistaken. The bullet whistled over his head and went through the canvas. A second shot tore into the wooden box beneath his feet, sending splinters of wood flying around his legs. Grabbing his own rifle, he leaped from the seat and, clattering to the ground, took shelter behind the iron wheel. He heard movement within the wagon and yelled at the girl to lie flat. At the same instant another shot rang out and ricocheted off the iron of the wheel on the other side of where he was crouched. Whoever was firing didn't appear to be too accurate. Raising his Sharps, he fired in the direction from which the shots had come. Straining his eyes, he caught a flash of red among some boulders. Something triggered in his mind. Where had he seen that red before? Who would be so inexpert as to reveal their presence? In a moment he thought he knew who it was.

'Bruford!' he shouted. 'Is that you?'

By way of reply another shot sent reverberations round the hillside and tore through the canvas high over his head.

'Bruford, it's me, Kramer! Stop shootin'!'

There was a moment's silence and then the voice of the oldster called out in response.

'Kramer? How do I know you ain't lyin'?'

'Just hold your fire. I'll step right out in the open and you can see for yourself.'

'Make sure you ain't got no gun in your hand!'

Kramer threw the rifle to one side and stepped from the shelter of the wagon. He knew he was taking a risk – he couldn't be completely sure it was the old-timer. For a moment he felt a tingling in his spine as he stood exposed to whoever was concealed among the rocks, but it was short-lived. The next moment there was a loud cry of 'Kramer!' and two figures emerged from cover – Bruford and his wife.

'Kramer!' Bruford called. 'What the hell are you doin' ridin' the wagon?'

They came sliding and slithering down the hillside

and came up to Kramer puffing and blowing with the effort.

'Good to see you,' Kramer exclaimed, and before he could add anything else he was seized by Clara and enfolded in her arms which clamped themselves round his waist. For a small woman of her years, she was surprisingly strong. When she let him go at last he could see tears in her eyes.

'Mr Kramer, who would have expected it?' she stammered.

Jess seemed to have recovered his senses.

'Any signs of the outcasts?' he said.

Kramer gestured towards the wagon.

'Got one in there,' he replied. 'She's young and she's had a rough time of it.'

Clara made for the wagon.

'Poor dear,' she said. 'Let me see what I can do.'

Holding open the flap of the wagon at the back, she climbed on board. Kramer and Jess Bruford could hear her moving about inside and making comforting noises.

'Your young lady will be OK now,' Bruford said. 'Clara'll be in her element now. She'll see to her.'

Kramer felt a huge wave of relief surge over him. He had done what he could and now he could hand over responsibility for Bonny Lange. At the same time he had found his friends and they appeared to be safe and well.

Later, when the introductions and explanations had been made, Kramer and Bruford sat down to discuss their next move.

'I guess there ain't any choice but to go back to town,' Bruford said.

'Won't that be a mite too risky? This character King seems to have had you in his sights already. He won't have taken kindly to you killing two of his men.'

Bruford looked surprised.

'Killed two of his men?' he repeated. 'I ain't killed two of his men. There was more of 'em than I reckoned to handle. Me and Clara just done and hid ourselves when we saw 'em comin.'

'But I found two bodies in the wagon,' Kramer said. 'I assumed it was your doin'. Who else could it have been?'

The oldster shook his head.

'Don't know,' he replied, 'but it sure weren't us.'

Kramer thought it over.

'Maybe they had a squabble among themselves,' Bruford continued. 'Or maybe it was one of the people we've been lookin' for.'

'Could be,' Kramer replied. 'But in that case, why would they have left the provisions?'

He thought for a moment.

'One thing though. If it wasn't you shot 'em, then maybe King won't be quite so ready to seek you out. Maybe it would be OK for you to return to town.'

'We could ride in kinda discreet,' Bruford said. 'Maybe real early before anyone's around to even notice us.'

'How would you feel about lookin' after the girl?' Kramer said.

'How do you mean?'

'Well, having thrown her out once, I don't suppose King would be too pleased to see her back again.'

A smile spread across Bruford's face.

'Now I wonder if you've got a particular reason for watchin' out for that young lady?' he mused. 'She sure is a pretty little thing.'

Kramer started to reply but found himself at a loss for the appropriate words.

'Don't you worry none,' Bruford said. 'We'll take care of Miss Lange and nobody won't know a thing. Even if King weren't involved, I reckon you'd have a job on your hands tryin' to prise the young lady away. Her and Clara seemed to be real pards already.'

They paused and sat silent, watching the slow flakes of snow descend. In the back of the wagon they could hear Clara and Miss Lange talking quietly together.

'What about you?' Bruford said.

'I'll come back with you, get myself sorted out and then take off for the mountains again. This time I won't bother with wagons or pack-horses. If those folk are still alive, they need to be found quick. I'll take what supplies I can and then find what I need up there.'

'Yeah. I guess you can live off the land pretty good.'

'Done it plenty of times before. There'll be plenty

of water up there anyways.'

He thought for a moment.

'Might be a good idea to make a cache of some of the stuff you brought with you in the wagon,' he said.

Bruford nodded.

'Should have thought of that myself,' he replied. 'Here, let me give you a hand.'

Together they unloaded some of the supplies and stored them beneath a rock, covering them with snow.

'Reckon you'll be able to find 'em again?' the oldster said.

Kramer nodded.

'Sure. Just hope the coyotes don't find 'em first.'

'You take care. Remember what happened to us. I don't know just what King's game is, but he seems to have men everywhere.'

'At least I won't have you gunnin' for me,' Kramer replied. 'And that sure is a big relief.'

CHAPTER THREE

Zebulon Ezekiel King had a name like an Old Testament prophet and he had the looks to match. On top of his large bulky frame was set a craggy face with a flowing black beard and bushy eyebrows. He had indeed caught religion, but so far it had been only as it suited his purposes and those purposes were coming along very nicely. He had control over the town and what he didn't already own he was well on the way to owning. The town was now named after him and he possessed a big swathe of the territory as well. The days when Kingsville had been a hick settlement in the middle of nowhere were fast coming to an end. Now there was talk of gold in the mountains and pretty soon he reckoned the town would be a jumping off point for hordes of miners avid to seek their fortunes. It didn't matter that most of the talk had been initiated and propagated by himself. Word caught on quick and now there was even a prospect of the railroad companies extending their reach into the area. If so, he was set to make a fortune in selling his land for rights of way. Sitting on the pillared veranda of his ranch-house, a glass of the finest single malt by his side and a fat cigar in his mouth, he had every right to feel pleased with himself. Maybe he would go into politics. He had the means to swing the vote his way. All in all, there was no end to the prospects opening before him. It didn't matter how he had got to where he was or what methods he might need to employ in future to maintain his power and control. Once you got to a certain high point, nobody asked questions about how you got there.

Looking up, he saw a rider approach. It was one of his employees, a man by the name of Rincorn. Riding into the yard, he swung down from the saddle.

'Well,' King said. 'I trust you got rid of those two trouble makers?'

The man grinned.

'Sure did. Took care of another bit of business at the same time.'

'Yeah? And what would that be?'

'You know that old ostler Bruford? Well, we come across him and his wife takin' a ride in a wagon.'

'Bruford?'

'Yeah, the oldster down at the livery stables. Him and his old woman never took too kindly to payin' up protection money. Anyway, we found 'em and gave 'em a bit of a scare. I think they'll maybe think differently in future, that is if they ever make it back to town. Done jumped clean off the wagon seat when they spotted us. Figure they're takin' a long walk through the snow right now.'

'Spare me the details,' King said. 'The thing is, you removed Tate and Watson? They were beginnin' to get ideas above their station.'

'You won't have no further trouble, boss.'

'Good. Once you've seen to the horse, why don't you join me? We'll go inside. Gettin' a little cold despite the brazier.'

The man led his horse towards the stables. He was thinking of Tate and Watson. He didn't know what they had done to rile King, but it probably wasn't much. King wasn't the sort of man to mess with and he, for one, thought he knew which side his bread was buttered.

While the snow had more or less ceased in the region of Kingsville, up in the mountains it was falling heavily. The little group of outcasts was in a bad way and Armitage knew that if they didn't find the cabin soon, they were doomed. The remaining girls were badly affected but one of the men was in an even worse condition, having been in an already depleted state from drink and the effects of his vagabond life on the streets of Kingsville. He was shivering violently and coughing up a vile substance laced with blood. There was another more personal reason why they needed to find the cabin. Although he had acquiesced to leaving Bonny Lange behind under protest, he nevertheless felt responsible for what had happened. In this he had surprised himself, not suspecting that he had the capacity for such a feeling. But there it was, unexpected but insistent. He had a gnawing sense of guilt about the affair and the quicker the rest of them were under some kind of shelter, the quicker he could go back to search for her. Not that they hadn't had good reason to leave Bonny Lange behind. He had tried carrying her but after a time had had to admit that he just didn't have the strength required. He had cursed himself for his weakness. Miss Tilly had been the one person who seemed to understand something of his feelings.

'It ain't your fault,' she had said. 'You did your best. We both did our best, you and me, but we had no choice. We had to give way to the others.'

Miss Tilly had been the only other person to raise any objections to leaving the girl behind. The girls had made a show of protesting, but they were weak and exhausted and there were cogent arguments against staying with the injured girl or slowing their already slow pace to try and bring her with them. It was urgent that they press on and she had been unable to walk. But Armitage was determined to go back and find her. He only hoped that he could find his way back to the spot and that she would still be alive when he got there. They were high in the mountains now and Armitage had a nagging feeling that they had taken the wrong course. He had little faith that they would find the hut or that it even existed. It might be a figment of Bentner's imagination. Even if he had lived in it, that was some time ago and the place might no longer be there or be inhabitable if it was. More than likely the man had no idea where it was and they were headed on a wild goose chase.

The route was becoming almost impassable. Across the path an outcrop of rock jutted out from the mountainside and the trail took a sharp left hand turn. Slithering and sliding through the snow, following one another in single file as the path narrowed, they struggled round the obstruction. To their left the mountain fell away in a sheer drop. On a clear day the view would be splendid but on this occasion it was obscured by the falling snow and by dark clouds which hung low and swirled like mist around the mountain. Armitage could see little ahead of him. It was a question of just struggling on, laboriously placing one foot in front of the other. At times his leg sank into the snow almost up to his knees, at others, where the snow lay over some raised rocky ground, it barely covered his ankles. He held his head down against the wind. Halting in his tracks, he looked back to see that he had got a little ahead of the others who were struggling up behind him. He started again, knowing that apart from any other consideration it was important that they keep moving. And then he saw it. Off the trail they were following, built under an overhang of the rocky cliff face, stood a cabin. His heart thumped. So Bentner was right. The place did exist after all. Turning, he started back down the track to tell the others.

'It's here! We've found it!'

His shouts were carried away on the wind but as they got nearer and saw his animated gestures, the others began to understand.

'The cabin! Come on! We've found it.'

He started back up the trail and then, turning off, felt himself floundering in deeper snow. Picking himself up, he struggled on till he was at the door of the cabin. Pulling and pushing, he tried to open it but it was jammed. Frantically he started to dig at the snow. The others, joining him, began to do the same. After a time they had partially cleared a space in front of the door and he began to tug at it again and this time it opened a little and then a little more. With a final effort he managed to open it sufficiently for them to enter. The first thing he noticed was that there was a pile of snow in one corner and looking up, saw that the roof was open at that point. But it was only there; the rest of it seemed sound enough. The cabin was bare. The only pieces of furniture were a table, a couple of rickety looking chairs and a broken down dresser which stood in the opposite corner to where the snow had drifted. The windows were empty but most of them still had wooden shutters which hung from their frames. Beside a narrow hearth something stood in a dark pile and when Armitage's eyes had grown accustomed to the gloom, he saw that it was a pile of wood. For the second time his heart thumped. This was almost too good to be true. There was a door at the back and walking through, Armitage found a second room with a bunk bed and a shelf. There were no windows because the back wall was the rock face of the mountain itself; the cabin had been built right against the mountain side.

Returning to the main room, he found the others sitting and lying in various attitudes of exhaustion.

'Come on,' he said, 'let's see if we can get a fire started.'

He went outside to gather some smaller twigs and branches from the scattered bushes and clumps of brush which poked out from the snow. He began to pull and tug and then he heard a voice behind him. It was Miss Tilly.

'Go easy,' she said. 'To work up a sweat wouldn't be a good idea.'

She joined him and when they had gathered a couple of armfuls they went back inside. Armitage had his matches in an inside pocket and soon had a fire taking hold. He gathered snow and put on a pot of coffee. They still had some food left from the bundle which Armitage had been loath to leave behind. Despite his tiredness he had carried it all the way.

'I'll see to that,' Miss Tilly said and began to try and rouse her two girls to help. Armitage felt a sudden surge of hope and a restitution of his usually ebullient spirits.

'Well, my friends,' he said. 'We may lack some of the comforts of the Golden Garter but as hostelries go, we could do worse.'

Bentner leered up at him from the floor.

'What did I tell you?' he said. 'You didn't believe me but here we are.'

'Very true, my man. I must say I did entertain some doubts as to the advisability of following such course of action as you indicated, but events have justified the faith we were reluctant to place in you.'

'You talk too much.'

'A very justifiable observation which in this instant I shall take measures to correct. *Fare fac.* Miss Tilly, how is that bacon doing?'

Carrying out the plan they had made, Kramer and the Brufords arrived back in town just as dawn was breaking. They came in the same way they had left, avoiding the main streets, and they met nobody. While Kramer and Bruford saw to the wagon and the horses, Clara helped the girl inside and installed her in a soft bed after providing her with some clean night clothes. Neither woman was very tall and they fitted surprisingly well. When daylight came Clara intended getting the doctor to take a look at Bonny's ankle. He was a good man and could be relied on to give nothing away to Marshal McLaren. When they had finished their respective tasks, they sat down to a good breakfast after which Kramer began to make his preparations for returning to the mountains.

'You'd better take some rest yourself,' Clara Bruford remarked.

Kramer was keen to get back on the trail but he was feeling very tired and saw the sense of her remark.

'That's not a bad idea. Reckon I might take a little siesta,' he said.

The girl had been placed in his room so he lay down on the couch. He could hear the Brufords moving about and then he remembered nothing more till he was rudely awakened by someone shaking his shoulder.

'Kramer,' Bruford said in his ear. 'I just ran back from town. The marshal's headed this way.'

In an instant Kramer was alert. Buckling his gun belt, he made for the door.

'Out this way,' Bruford said, indicating the back entrance.

Kramer swiftly moved to the stable and fixed his saddle. Springing to the pinto's back, he rode it down the runway. The Brufords were standing together.

'It might be nothin',' Jess said. 'But I figure it might be a good idea for you to git out of here.'

'What about you?' Kramer said.

'Don't worry about us. We've got used to handlin' the marshal. It won't be us he's concerned about.'

'And the girl?'

Clara Bruford summoned a smile.

'She'll be fine. Stop arguin' and get goin'.'

Kramer hesitated a moment and then touched his spurs to the horse's flanks.

'I'll be back,' he called as the pinto broke into a trot. Soon he was away from the town and in the open country where he drew rein, uncertain whether to continue or go back. Then he reckoned the Brufords could handle things with the marshal. He might be awkward but the Brufords had been around a long time and were well respected in town. It couldn't be to the marshal's benefit to do anything too drastic with regard to them for the moment. Kramer had no doubt that the marshal was in King's pay and that neither of them would hesitate to strike if they thought it was necessary and the moment was at hand. But that moment wasn't yet. Maybe the marshal would not bother with him either, but it seemed quite likely that he might end up in the jailhouse at the very least. McLaren had been suspicious of him from the start. He thought about the castaways at the mercy of the elements in the mountains. He was their only chance of survival. He needed to stay free and he needed to get moving quickly. Already he regretted that catnap but together with the breakfast it had done him a lot of good. Without further hesitation he urged the pinto forward.

When he reached the spot where he had cached the food, he stopped to check that it was still there. It was just as he and Bruford had left it. Mounting the pinto, he continued up the trail. The weather was bleak and desolate and as he rode the snow began to fall heavily. There was little chance that he would find any sign so he figured to keep heading higher on the assumption that the refugees would have continued that way. Once he was above the tree line, as dark began to descend once more he found a spot that was comparatively sheltered and built a fire, rubbing down the pinto with some evergreen needles before feeding it. As night deepened the cold became severe but it didn't bother him. He was used to it, used to riding the wild and hostile trails in high country just as much as in the lowlands. He drank coffee laced with whiskey and some food. Towards midnight the snow stopped and the clouds parted to reveal a huge open patch of sky littered with stars. They seemed low enough to touch. Checking his horse for a final time, he stretched out beneath his blankets and prepared to sleep. He was beginning to nod off when suddenly his eyes flicked open and he sat up, reaching for his gun. He listened closely for any sound. He couldn't be sure he had heard anything and there was nothing he could detect, but he still had an uneasy feeling that someone was nearby. He looked towards the horse. It gave no evidence of having been disturbed. Getting to his feet and throwing a few extra twigs on to the dwindling fire, he moved off to one side and from the cover of the shadows peered into the darkness beyond the reach of the flames. He held his gaze for a long time but there was no indication of movement. Gun in hand, he moved out into the blackness, moving forward slowly and silently, his senses alert, circling about the camp he had made. Looking back, he could see the firelight like a tiny beacon of hope on the cold and inhospitable mountainside. He made his way back, whispering a few words to the horse as he passed before resuming his place just beyond the reach of the firelight. He watched and listened for a while longer before settling into an uneasy slumber.

The dawn came slowly and Kramer made himself some coffee before saddling up once more and riding out into the cold early light. The frozen snow lay deep across the landscape, obliterating landmarks and staring back at the lowering sky with empty eyes. The pinto picked its way forward and they made slow progress. Then Kramer's eyes picked out something against the white background. At first he took no notice, assuming it was a rock or the topmost branches of a bush poking through the snow. The pinto's ears were pricked up. Dropping from the saddle, Kramer started to walk across the intervening ground, slipping and sliding and falling into drifts that reached to his waist. When he was still a little distance away he could see that the black object was not a branch or a boulder, but the inert figure of a man. Struggling through the snow, he reached the man at last. He was lying on his back and already the snow had drifted over a part of him. It was lucky that the snowfall had relented during the night or he would have been covered. He wore a thick coat over a black suit but it had evidently been borrowed because it did not fit his lanky frame. Kramer bent down and put his ear next to the man's mouth. He was still breathing. Opening the flask he carried with him, Kramer propped the man up and poured some drops of whiskey down his throat. It seemed a hopeless task. It was a miracle that the man had survived at all. It was too much to expect that he might yet pull through, Suddenly the man's ice-encrusted eyes opened and he looked at Kramer.

'I'd have preferred a Kentucky bourbon but beggars can't be choosers.'

Kramer was taken aback.

'Give me another swig,' the man said, 'and I might be sufficiently recovered to be able to sit up.'

He swallowed another few drops and then pulled Kramer's hand so the bottle tipped a little more. When he had finished he gasped and then faintly smiled.

'Whoever you are, I can't say how relieved I am to make your acquaintance,' he murmured. 'The name is Reynard Armitage and I believe you have saved my life.'

'Hal Kramer,' Kramer replied, 'and I wouldn't bank on that just yet.'

'I saw a fire. I tried to reach it.'

'You almost did,' Kramer replied. 'Let's try and get you back there.'

Going down on one knee, he lifted the man in his arms and carried him back to the horse where he slung him over the saddle. Mounting up, he rode back to the camp and set about rebuilding the fire. The man had lost consciousness and Kramer laid him gently down near the flames, covering him with blankets. He was pretty far gone and Kramer wasn't convinced that he would come round again, but after a few hours the man's eyes flickered open and he looked around.

'Here, take this,' Kramer said, proffering a tin mug of steaming black coffee. He had made it extra strong even by his own standards and it would have lifted the hide off a steer. When he had drunk it the man sat up.

'You haven't seen any sign of a young lady?' he asked.

Kramer was surprised by the note of anxiety in the man's voice. For someone who had come through an ordeal like he had, it was unexpected.

'If you mean Bonny Lange, yeah, I found her and she's safe.'

'Thank heavens,' the man said. 'It seems I have even more to thank you for.'

'I know your story,' Kramer said. 'At least enough of it. What about the rest of you folks? Are they still alive?'

It was the gambler's turn to be surprised.

'They were alive when I left them,' he said. 'I think they're safe for the moment but they can't hold out for long.'

'Then we'd better find them just as quick as you're

able to hang on to a horse,' Kramer said. 'Think you can find your way back to wherever they are?'

The man nodded.

'I believe I can show you the way,' he said. 'We found an old cabin further up the mountain.'

'Just you rest up a while and then we'll make a move,' Kramer said.

The man threw aside the blanket and, wobbling, succeeded in getting to his feet.

'I'm OK now. As you intimated, we'd best find them speedily.'

Kramer quickly put out the fire and they mounted the pinto. Kramer was impressed by the speed of the man's recovery. He was obviously in some difficulties and quite weak, but Kramer reflected that beneath it all he must have the constitution of a bull buffalo. As they rode out of camp, the snow began to fall.

It didn't take long to reach the cabin but when they got there it was already too late for the man with the cough. The first thing Kramer had to do was to bury him nearby.

'Anyone know his name?' he asked.

Tilly Lush provided the information and Kramer carved it on a piece of board – Jim Radford. For years he had been a familiar sight on the streets of Kingsville but no one had known him other than by his soubriquet of Polecat.

'That board won't stay for long,' Kramer remarked.

'Long enough for him to be remembered as the

first of us to die,' Tilly replied.

She turned to Kramer.

'It's only thanks to you that Bonny and the gambler are still around,' she added.

The two girls were in a bad way and it was obvious that everyone needed food. Kramer rode down the mountain and finding the cache, returned with it to the cabin. When he got back he set about making repairs to the shack so that by the time he had finished it was almost comfortable. The weather had improved a little. Although the cold was relentless the skies cleared and there were no further falls of snow. In his endeavours he was assisted by Miss Tilly and then by Armitage, who had made a full recovery from his ordeal. The supplies would not last indefinitely, so one morning Kramer rode off in search of game. Without him, the outcasts would have died of starvation, but to his practised eyes the mountain country offered relatively easy pickings. He hadn't ridden too far when he detected signs of mountain lion. He knew they lived off elk and deer. Riding an isolated trail which had probably originally been made by Indians or mountain men, he found a group of deer bunched together. They were not nervous because nobody ever used the trail and it was easy to shoot one and then dress and skin it. While he was busy with this he looked about him. It was a wide, big country with forested slopes giving way to timberline and then the soaring, lonely peaks etched in jagged, serrated edges against the sky. It was wild and empty but he kept a lookout for sign of King's men. He didn't expect to find any and he was not disappointed. Still he found himself wondering about those two bodies he had found in the Brufords's wagon. If the Brufords hadn't killed them, then who had? He also found himself wondering about what to do next. Unless the little group gathered at the cabin moved out pretty soon, they would be stuck there when the winter really set in. But where would they move to? The only real option was the town and there was no prospect that King would simply sit by and watch them return. Although they could prove no real threat to him, he couldn't afford to let his authority be undermined. The more he reflected on the matter, the more it seemed they would have to see out the winter at the cabin. Entry and exit would become impossible when the snows blocked the passes and the trails. He himself might be able to move about and perhaps maintain contact with the Brufords and with whatever might be happening in town, but even that would be difficult. But what would happen when spring arrived? They couldn't stay in the mountains for ever; they would have to move sometime. One thing he didn't consider was moving on himself. When he arrived in Kingsville he had no intention of staying long; now things had changed. He didn't take to being bossed around by King and his acolytes and he had a strong objection to seeing innocent people being bullied. Besides, he had a personal interest in it now, and it wasn't just

Bonny Lange he was thinking of. He had no inkling of what he expected to happen or how things might pan out, but he had a notion that a day would come when it would be either him or King. And King held all the aces.

The next day threatened a storm and Kramer decided to pay a visit to town. He wasn't anxious about the Brufords but was curious to know how they were doing. If he didn't take the opportunity, they were liable to be snowed in and it might not be easy to get another chance. As he rode down the mountain the snow began to fall; the trail became extremely difficult and when he reached the plank bridge over the stream it was to find the water frozen solid. As he approached his attention was drawn to something flapping in the breeze. It was a poster fastened to the town sign. Reaching out, he tore it down and was taken aback to find that it was a Wanted poster with his own name on it: *Wanted in connection with murder. Hal Kramer. $500 reward.*

'Looks like we got even more trouble,' he said to the horse.

He looked about him but there was nothing to be seen except the driving snow. All the same he figured it might be wise to leave the pinto and proceed on foot. Leading it to the shelter of some trees, he hobbled it and then made his way across the plank bridge. When he reached the outskirts of town he took a back way, looking out for anybody. It wasn't likely there would be too many people about and even if he ran into someone it was unlikely they would recognize him. Pulling his hat lower and the collar of his jacket higher, he came to the back of the livery stable and knocked on the door of the house. There was no answer and Kramer was beginning to feel concerned when suddenly the window curtain was drawn aside and the lined face of Clara Bruford appeared. For a moment she looked at him with worry in her eyes and then she recognized him. In a moment the bolt was drawn and he was welcomed into the kitchen.

'Jess!' she shouted, 'Look who's here.'

In a moment the figure of Jess appeared in the doorway and behind him another face, that of Bonny Lange.

'Man!' Jess exclaimed, 'It sure is good to see you. Don't stand there, step right inside.'

Kramer moved through to the main room where he took of his coat and hat.

'Sit down. Jess, pour the man a drink. You must be hungry. I'll rassle somethin' up.'

'It's OK,' Kramer began, but she was already back in the kitchen.

'How are you, Mr Kramer?' a gentle voice murmured.

Kramer turned to Bonny. She was looking quite different from the last time he had seen her. He had not realized how beautiful she was. Instead of the gaudy silk outfit she now wore a blue checked gingham dress and her hair hung in loose waves to her shoulders.

'I'm fine, ma'am. And you sure look good.'

Kramer couldn't be certain, but he thought he detected a slight blush.

'Did you find the others?' Jess intervened.

'Yep, I found them. Right now they're keepin' safe in a cabin way up in the mountains. What about the situation down here?'

Jess looked slightly uncomfortable. Kramer drew the tattered wet poster from his pocket.

'So you've seen that?'

'Five hundred dollar reward. They could at least have priced me a bit higher! What's it all about?'

'Shortly after you left, the marshal turned up. It was just as well you made a quick getaway. He was lookin' to put you under arrest for the murder of those two men you found in the wagon, the ones you thought me and Clara might have done for.'

'Why would he do that?'

'No doubt King's behind it. We both know you had nothin' to do with killin' those two *hombres*, but I guess it's just convenient for King to blame you for it.'

'I've never met King.'

'You've riled the marshal and he will have had words with King. The mere suspicion that you might have helped those castaways is sufficient for him to want to have you out of the way. One of his men might try to do it. This way he'll have any reward seeker with an itchy trigger finger on your trail.'

'What about you and Clara?'

'We're small fry. He might suspect we were out in that wagon carryin' supplies for the outcasts but he can't be sure. He knows that if he acts against us he might upset some of the townsfolk. Not that he would let it worry him too much. We just ain't one of his priorities.'

'That might change if King finds out about Bonny.'

Bonny looked up in alarm.

'I don't want to put you folks into any danger,' she said. 'You've done enough for me already. I could move on.'

She turned to Kramer.

'Maybe I should come back with you to the cabin,' she said.

Jess had poured Kramer a stiff glass of whiskey and now poured one for himself.

'Don't you go frettin' none, ma'am,' he said. 'Me and Clara is plumb glad to have you with us. We wouldn't hear of you headin' back up that mountain.'

'Jess is right,' Kramer said. 'Things up there are too crowded anyway and the weather is really settin' in. If it's OK with Jess and Clara, this is the place for you. At least for the time bein'.'

Just then Clara came into the room carrying a tray.

'What's that you been saying?'

She laid the tray beside Kramer.

'We was thinkin' that you might stay here yourself,' she said. 'There's plenty of room and between the house and the stable there's lots of places you could hide if the marshal ever comes knockin'.'

Kramer picked up his knife and fork and set about the steak and potatoes Clara had prepared.

'I sure appreciate the offer,' he said, 'but King has ratcheted up the stakes now he's made me an outlaw. Now I know you folks are gettin' along down here, I think the best thing for me is to stay clear of the marshal and not take chances bein' seen around town. Besides, the folks up in the cabin will be needin' me.'

'Somethin's gotta give,' Jess said. 'Things can't go on like this much longer.'

Kramer turned to him.

'Who do you think was behind the shootin' of those two men?' he said.

Jess downed his drink.

'Well,' he answered, 'I guess you've raised an interestin' point there. Seems to me that it must have been King's own men. Now if that's the case, maybe it signifies that all is not completely well in the King domain.'

'How do you mean?'

Think about it. Two of King's men are killed by another of King's *hombres.* What does that suggest to you?'

Kramer finished the last of his meal, mopping up the gravy with a thick slice of bread.

'I see what you mean. Actually the same thought had occurred to me. Maybe there is dissent in King's camp; perhaps he's not got full control. Maybe there's a rival faction. Even if it doesn't go that far, he could be having some difficulties maintaining his position.'

'I figure it that way, although if there's any internal opposition I would guess it's only minor. King is just too powerful for anyone to seriously mount a challenge.'

'Still, it may be the chink in his armour we're lookin' for.'

Kramer paused, thinking hard.

'Somethin' else,' he continued. 'When those folks were stranded in the mountains, somebody left them a bag of supplies. Don't sound like the sort of thing King would do. So who was behind it?'

'I guess that must have been the deputy marshal,' Clara said.

'Riff Rogers?'

'Yes. I know Jess ain't got a lot of time for him, but he ain't so bad.'

'If you're right, that could give us some extra leverage.'

Jess looked closely at Kramer.

'You talk as if you got some sort of feud with King.'

Kramer smiled grimly.

'Before, it was because I chose to go against him. Now it looks like I ain't got no choice anyway.'

Kramer got to his feet and moved towards the door.

'I ain't sure how things are likely to be fixed for

awhiles. It's goin' to be hard up in the mountains and maybe there won't be any way I can get down here. Besides, I got a price on my head.'

Clara came up to him and put her arms round him.

'Just you take care', she said. 'And don't worry none about Miss Bonny. She'll be safe here.'

When she had released him he shook hands with Jess.

'We're here when you want us,' he said.

Kramer turned to the girl. Both of them were suddenly awkward. Kramer held out his hand and she took it. Looking into her eyes, he smiled and they held hands for just a little longer than was necessary.

'Please be careful,' she said, repeating Clara's words. 'Please come back to us.'

Kramer nodded and then moved quickly to the door. He went out and passed though the corrals without looking back. The snow was thick now as he walked down the lane. The wind was blowing it into his face and he bent over, leaning against it, his hat pulled low over his eyes. Nearing the end of town, he didn't notice two figures coming towards him. They were almost upon him when he was brought to a sudden stop as a rough voice called out:

'Kramer! You're goin' the wrong way. Jail's thataway!'

Kramer looked up quickly. Through the blinding snow he could see the two men standing in his path with their guns drawn. He didn't wait for any further talk. In an instant his six-gun was in his hand and spitting flame and lead. The man on the right wheeled back, his gun flying from his hand. At the same time the other man fired and as Kramer hurled himself face forward into the snow he felt a tug of wind as the bullet flew past where he had just been standing. Taking a fraction of a moment to take aim, he pulled the trigger and saw his attacker stagger backwards. He fired again and the man fell to his knees before slumping to the ground. The other man was facing him with his hands in the air.

'Don't shoot!' he shouted.

Kramer got to his feet. The man's second gun was still in its gun belt.

'Throw it down!' Kramer called. 'Butt first.'

The man reached for his gun and made to cast it aside when suddenly it spun in his hand and the muzzle was pointed towards Kramer. The man fired almost at the same instant as Kramer but it wasn't Kramer who went down. The sounds of firing were succeeded by an eerie silence as Kramer bent down to examine the bodies which were bleeding into the snow. One glance was sufficient to tell him that they were both dead. There was little doubt in his mind that they belonged to King's outfit. They had the look, even in death, of men who made a living by their guns. Holstering his own weapons, Kramer took off at a run past the last few houses, not caring to become embroiled in further gunplay or complications that might be to the detriment of the Brufords or to the people depending on him at the cabin. The snow dragged at his legs but he made it to the bridge without further encounter. Climbing into leather, he turned the pinto towards the mountains, knowing the marshal would soon be on his trail with an official posse ahead of King's other gunslicks who wouldn't be far behind.

CHAPTER FOUR

It was late at night when Kramer stopped to make camp in the foothills. The climb had been slow and arduous and not just because of the weather. Every now and again Kramer had stopped to check his back trail and waited till he was completely satisfied there was no one following him. By the time he had found a suitable camping spot, he felt pretty sure that he was safe for the time being and that there would be no pursuit till the following morning. Long before dawn had touched the peaks of the mountains he was on his way again. It wasn't too far to the cabin but the conditions were so bad, it was going to take a long time to get there. The pinto was a good mountain horse but it was finding it almost impossible to make its way through the snow and avoid slipping into the snowdrifts which were all around what had once been the trail. It was impossible now to pick it out. Kramer was relying on his eyes and his instincts to keep going and avoid disaster. Above him loomed the mountain but he could see nothing of it through the snow. He was cocooned in a still and claustrophobic world: the only sounds were the creaking of leather and the incessant whispering of the snow. At least, he reflected, it made it less likely that the posse would ever catch up with him.

The horse struggled on. Kramer was becoming a little soporific when suddenly another sound plucked at his drifting consciousness and he was instantly alert. It was an alien sound which he couldn't at first place, but then he realized what it was – the faint click of metal. Even as he wondered what anyone could be doing out here his instinctive reactions took over and he flung himself along the length of the horse, reaching for the saddle horn. The next moment there was a booming sound which echoed down the mountainside. The shot was quickly followed by another which went whistling close by his head. If the next one took his horse, he knew he was doomed; without it, he would stand little chance of survival. In a moment he had pulled hard at the reins and dragged the horse down, rolling away from it as it fell. The horse plunged into soft snow and for once Kramer was glad of it. Pulling the Sharps from its scabbard, he lay flat, mostly covered by snow, searching for any sign of his attacker. He had been bushwhacked but it had nothing to do with the shootout in Kingsville; whoever it was had already been on the mountain. So what did he have against Kramer? More relevant, who could it be? Through the driving snow his eyes searched the mountainside. There was nothing to be seen. Reaching up, he flung his hat into the air. As he had hoped, there was a responsive shot, sufficient for him to detect the flash of flame. Raising his rifle, he fired and then rolled away again as an answering shot kicked up the snow nearby. He was in a bad position and trying to work out his next move when a voice called out from higher up the mountain.

'Bentner! Put down the rifle!'

It was answered almost immediately by another shot and then, after a slight pause, a further shot rang out, this time less loud. There was a pause and then another crack echoed through the snowy air. Kramer remained flat while the snow drifted over him, waiting for somebody to make the next move. After a few moments it came as the voice he had heard called out again.

'Is that you, Kramer? It's Reynard Armitage!'

'What's goin' on?' Kramer called back.

'It's OK. It was Bentner shootin' at you. He went berserk. I'm afraid I had no option but to shoot him. I think he's dead.'

For a moment more Kramer hesitated before getting to his feet.

'Where are you, Armitage?'

'Go easy. I'm comin' down.'

A few minutes passed and then Kramer's straining eyes made out a dim shape slithering down the mountainside towards him. As it came closer he recognized the figure of the gambler.

'Kramer,' the man said. 'Let me apologize on behalf of us all. You could have been killed.'

'Guess it's me that owes you,' Kramer responded.

'Then we're equal,' Armitage replied.

'Yeah. This is kinda becomin' a habit. Tell me what happened.'

'After you left Bentner started acting strangely. His language was most offensive to the female element of our company. He found a rifle – there were a few weapons stashed away in a cupboard in the bedroom. When he left the cabin I thought it might be prudent to follow him. Lucky that rifle was an old .56 calibre Paterson and I happened to have my derringer.'

'Why would he want to dry-gulch me?'

'Who knows? Maybe he was after your horse.'

'Well, that's one less mouth to feed,' Kramer responded.

'We'd best be gettin' back,' Reynard said. 'The ladies are on their own.'

For the second time the pinto had to carry the two of them up the mountain but it soon became apparent that it was finding it too difficult. They both climbed down and Kramer led the horse, glancing all about him as he did so. The snow was creaking and groaning and he didn't like the look of things at all. Layers of fresh snow had fallen on the icy surface of previous layers and the whole thing was unstable. The way up the mountain became more and more treacherous and seemed to get longer rather than shorter the higher they climbed. There were no landmarks but they were sure they were getting close to the cabin when suddenly there came a roaring sound from over their heads. Looking quickly up, Kramer saw the top of the mountain detach itself and begin what seemed a slow descent like a tremendous waterfall that appears to move in slow motion when actually it is hurtling down at speed. The roaring sound grew in volume. Armitage was looking up also when Kramer's voice cut through his inertia.

'Avalanche!'

Ahead of them the cabin appeared round the bend in the path and as the snows began to descend upon them and the white side of the mountain slid in their direction, they made a desperate burst to reach it. It stood against the side of the mountain while the snows poured over it in a white cascade. Loosened by the snow, huge boulders and rocks were bumping down the mountainside and one went bouncing over their heads as, with a last effort, they reached the cabin door. It was flung open and Armitage staggered inside while Kramer sought the shelter of the overhang for the pinto. He stood there while the world seemed to reverberate with sound and motion as the torrents of snow streamed down and built themselves against the walls of the cabin. Then it was over. As quickly as it had begun the avalanche came to a halt and silence returned to the mountains. A mound of snow now separated Kramer from the front of the cabin. With some difficulty the door was pushed open sufficiently for Armitage and Miss Lush to help him remove the snow, so he was able to move the horse to shelter and attend to its needs before making his own way to the cabin. The three of them had to squeeze their way inside to where the girls were still cowering in terror.

'Well,' Kramer said. 'Looks like we're well and truly trapped here now.'

Miss Lush looked towards the windows but there was nothing to be seen except snow banked against them.

'At least we made ourselves as comfortable as we could,' she said.

She glanced towards the sobbing girls and the pile of wood which had been placed by the fireside.

'We have what we need. We got supplies and we got fuel. Later we'll dig a path through the snow outside and get down to the rest of those logs.'

'But the food won't last for long,' one of the girls expostulated. 'What'll we do when it runs out?'

'We got Mr Kramer with us. He'll find a way.'

She looked towards Kramer with a confident expression.

'Sure, we'll be OK,' he said. 'I'll go straight in to makin' myself a pair of snowshoes. I've been in worse situations than this. We'll just have to make the best of it. We'll get by.'

'And I think it's time we did us some cookin' right now, ain't that right girls? Mr Kramer must be needin' somethin'.'

Miss Lush led the girls into the kitchen.

'She's a good lady,' Armitage said. 'I don't know how those girls would have fared without her ministrations. I think she knew better than to ask questions right now about Bentner.'

'We're better off without him,' Kramer said. 'But at least he knew about this place. He done us a good turn there.'

Later, when he had eaten and warmed himself at the fire, Kramer felt better. He was safe himself now from pursuit. For the time being the cabin was inaccessible and the trails and passes through the mountains would be closed. He had no worries about finding food; he could provide for them. It would be difficult, but he could get around – he could survive in the mountains. But it was going to be a long wait and he was already missing a young woman in a blue checked gown who had looked with longing when he left the town. He hoped she would look at him that way when he returned.

Kramer had no concerns about Bonny's safety; King had no idea that she had escaped her fate on the mountain and was living with the Brufords. It was doubtful that he knew of her existence. King had other matters to concern him, the chief of them being the railroad concessions he had been counting on. He had heard from his lawyer that there were problems. The company which had been considering extending the line were having second thoughts and looking at another route. Talk of finding gold in the mountains had evaporated and unless something was done to revive interest, they would have no incentive to build the line in the direction of Kingsville. And that wasn't all. He had problems nearer to home. He had learned by hard experience that when a man reaches a position of power and influence, he arouses jealousy and opposition. There was murmuring among his own men and the steps he had taken so far to silence them had not been entirely effective. Some of the men were getting restless in any event. He had employed some of the most notorious gunslicks to carry out his orders, but there hadn't been enough action to keep them contented. He had himself partly to blame for this. In his campaign to keep the town quiet and eliminate any elements who might object to his high-handed control, he had created a monster of order and decorum which ill-fitted his men's requirements. He was something of a Puritan himself and it suited him to have shut the saloons and eradicated the drinking and gambling element but it had affected his own men. They had little or nothing to do of a night and since he was likely to need their services in future, it had become necessary to do something about it. He thought about the saloon which was standing empty. Maybe it was time to open it again. And if the possibilities for finding gold were revived, any prospectors attracted to the area would require entertainment. It didn't sit square on with his own strict leanings in that regard, but he couldn't afford to be too particular. Zebulon King was a strange man, a man of contradictions. In his lust for power it did not trouble his conscience to tread on anyone who got in his way, even to the extent of cold-blooded murder. But he had little sympathy or consideration for the normal peccadilloes of human behaviour. For all his wealth and influence he lived an austere life which was devoid of the companionship of women. He apparently lacked the basic emotions. To him a thing was either right or wrong and he it was who decided on the criteria. He was a hard man, not only on others but on himself, and all the more dangerous for being convinced of his own correctness.

So it was that the citizens of Kingsville awoke one morning to find workmen hard at it, busy replenishing the old Golden Garter. In a short time the work was completed and the place reopened as the Blue Bucket. The name was not accidental. By recalling the name of the old lost mine of that name King hoped to suggest the possible presence of gold in the mountains. Maybe some gullible fools would even equate it with the old mine even though that had amounted to nothing more than a creek bed a long way off in Oregon. It wasn't an easy matter to find staff and he almost regretted his decision to run the old habitués out of town. Still, there were others who had survived the purge and they would be sufficient till he brought in more. Soon the old place was almost back to its former glories, but with one difference. Behind it all loomed the granite figure of King keeping a check on any manifestation of what he would have termed loose behaviour. The bar was busy enough; poker and faro were revived and the roulette table spun, but there were no girls and no entertainment. There was no piano tinkling out songs for people to sing along to and the presence of King's most trusted lieutenants ensured that things were kept calm, even if it meant they had to enforce the rules and regulations against some of their own men. King was not averse to using hired guns, but the core of his support were people like himself, hard, inflexible men who had risen with King and were fiercely loyal to the brand. Or so they seemed.

The days passed and became weeks. Isolated in the mountain cabin, the outcasts succeeded in getting along. People adjust to circumstances and after a while the cramped living conditions became the norm. The girls were fortunate to have Tilly Lush to take care of them and she in turn was fortunate to have the company of Reynard Armitage. It soon became apparent to Kramer that there was something between them.

'She's a mighty fine woman,' Armitage confided in him, not for the first time. 'A mighty fine woman. It was a marvel how she used to run the Golden Garter. A man could do a lot worse than to negotiate a merger between his own enterprises and hers.'

'By which you mean hitch her wagon to yours?'

'An abused but apt metaphor. That would indeed be

a suitable alternative terminology. Back in Kentucky some folk might not appreciate her merits but it would only be to their detriment.'

'You hail from Kentucky?'

'Lexington, appropriately named the Athens of the West.'

'I don't know about that.'

'Athens, the centre of ancient Greek culture and democracy. Ah, the blue grass country. Have your travels taken you there?'

'Can't rightly be sure. I been around a lot of places, passin' through, some I never did catch the name of.'

'And I wonder if in your travels you ever came across a situation quite like the one which appertains here?'

'You referrin' to Zebulon King?'

'When I first visited these parts he was no more than a small rancher. Now it seems he holds the power of life and death over the whole territory.'

'Hasn't anybody stood up against him?'

'If they did they didn't live long. But howsoever that might be there are still a few folks who might be prepared to act against him.'

Kramer's thoughts turned to the Brufords. How many others were there like them?

'How about you?' Kramer said.

The gambler looked thoughtful.

'Mr Kramer, I was never a man given to violence, but in my professional capacities I have had occasion to deal with some tight situations. A man doesn't make a living with the cards without intermittent accusations of underhand dealings.'

'You mean cheating.'

'Call it what you will, it is an occupational hazard, although I may say I have never had recourse to such methods. The point is, Mr Kramer, that though my natural instincts tend to the pacific, circumstances might be such as would persuade me to forego them.'

'That's good to know,' Kramer said. 'That makes two of us.'

'I appreciate that the odds are long; this time it certainly isn't any kind of saddle-blanket gamble we'd be getting into. But then a timid heart never filled a flush.'

Just at that moment they were joined by Tilly who had entered from the back room and overheard the tail end of the conversation.

'Make that three,' she said. 'You seem to forget that I have a score to settle with Mr Zebulon King just as much as you.'

Kramer looked up at her and grinned.

'Three,' he said. 'And I sure would rather have you on my side than working for the opposition.'

'I can handle a gun,' she said. 'If it were ever to come to that.'

Kramer nodded.

'I'm afraid it sure looks that way.'

Tilly had made coffee and she poured it out.

'You know,' she said, 'goin' back to what you were sayin', I reckon there could be a lot more than the three of us.'

'That's kinda what we were discussin',' Kramer remarked.

'It takes a lot to stir up some folks, but there's people back in Dirt Crossing who've just had about had their fill of King and his high-handed ways. There's a heap of resentment built up over the years. Maybe it wouldn't take an awful lot to rally 'em round.'

Kramer took a mouthful of coffee and swallowed before looking up at the former proprietess of the Golden Garter.

'Do you reckon you could pick out the ones who might be prepared to do somethin' about King?'

She thought for a moment.

'Sure,' she said. 'Leastways I got a pretty good idea. I might be wrong about some of 'em but I think I know the townsfolk fairly well.'

She laughed.

'Maybe better than some of 'em would like.'

'Miss Lush has always been the acme of discretion,' Armitage said.

Kramer took another swallow.

'There's nothin' to be done for the moment,' he said, 'not till the weather breaks. But it might be real useful to have a list of those folks.'

'Certainly,' Tilly said. 'I could do that. I can introduce you to some of 'em.'

'That won't be possible,' Kramer replied. 'You'd be recognized the second you set foot in town. But I could sneak in without bein' spotted. And I could get down the mountain.'

'You intend making contact with those citizens?' Armitage said. 'Sound them out, as it were?'

'It might be a long shot, but it would be worth a try. To be honest, I'm gettin' to feel plumb hogtied stuck here.'

Tilly glanced in the direction of the two young ladies.

'Ain't the company good enough to keep you interested?'

'Company's fine,' Kramer replied. 'Just feel like I'm rustin' up is all. Need to cut the wolf loose.'

Tilly smiled.

'I got a feelin' Zebulon King ain't goin' to like that one bit when it happens,' she replied.

It was Sunday in Kingsville with the wind lashing sleet against the clapboard buildings. The morning service had just come to an end and people were streaming out of the church under the watchful gaze of some of King's henchmen. A couple of them drifted away in the direction of the livery stables and began knocking hard on the door of the Bruford house. Seeing them coming from an upstairs window, Clara quickly moved to Bonny's room.

'Quick!' she said. 'Come with me.'

'What is it?' Bonny replied, seeing the look of urgency on Clara's face.

'A couple of King's men are headed this way and I don't like the look of it. I recognize one; he's called Rincorn and he's a real mean son of a bitch.'

They clattered down the stairs and out the back door. With a quick look to the right and left, Clara led Bonny to the stables where Jess was feeding the horses.

'Hello,' he said, 'have you—?'

He stopped whatever he had been going to say when he saw the concern on their faces.

'Rincorn and another of King's men are headed this way. Go back and stall them if you can.'

Jess didn't need further information. In a trice he was through the stable door and back in the house. There was a ladder standing against the wall and motioning to Bonny to help her, Clara quickly stood it in the centre of the stable so that it leaned against a trapdoor leading to an attic where Jess stored hay and some of his tools. Bonny made to climb the ladder but Clara shook her head.

'That's to put them off. You go down here.'

Pushing aside some of the hay littering the place, she revealed an iron ring let into the floor at which she tugged. With a little effort it came up to reveal a flight of steps descending into a dark shaft.

'Quickly, down you go.'

Bonny hesitated but Clara tried to reassure her.

'It's OK. There's only a few steps and there's candles and matches down there.'

For a moment longer Bonny held back and then at

Clara's urging put her foot on the first step. The place looked dark and forbidding but as Clara had said, there were not many steps. When she reached the bottom she found herself in a small space which someone had made an effort to make almost habitable. There was a chair and a small table on which stood candles and matches. Nailed to the wall was a rough shelf on which stood some books.

'Are you all right down there?' Clara called.

'Yes, I think so.'

'Don't worry. I'll be back before long. It's just a precaution.'

With that she replaced the ring and Bonny suddenly felt a wave of panic as the daylight was extinguished and she stood in the dark. She made to move back up the stairs but had got no further than the second step when there came a bumping sound from overhead. She stopped and then slowly continued her progress. She sensed rather than saw the entrance above her but when she reached up and began to push, there was no movement. She guessed that the sound she had heard was Clara moving something into place to cover the existence of the ring. Again she felt a surge of fear clutch at her stomach but recalling Clara's words she fought to control herself and made her way steadily back down the stairway. Already her eyes were adjusting to the gloom and, making her way to the table, she lit a couple of the candles, placing them in empty bottles which had been left for the purpose. It didn't seem so bad and she knew she could rely on the Brufords. Making her way to the shelf she looked at what she had thought were books to find they weren't books but mail-order catalogues of various types; for clothing, stock and implements. Picking one out, she sat down at the table and began to thumb it through.

When Jess Bruford opened the door to Rincorn and the other man he had no chance to do as Clara had suggested – no sooner had he opened it a fraction than they burst through into the living room. Jess followed close behind.

'Kinda unfriendly way to pay a visit,' he said.

The two men looked at him hard. They were tough types, each of them wearing two guns tied by thongs.

'It ain't no social call,' Rincorn snarled.

Jess moved towards the kitchen.

'Perhaps I can offer you boys a cup of coffee,' he said.

Rincorn stepped forward and stood in his way.

'No coffee, granddad,' he said. 'Just pay up and we'll be gone.'

Jess stroked his stubbled chin.

'Now there you got me,' he said. 'The thing is, I been thinkin' I done enough of handin' money over to Mr King. Besides I just ain't got it.'

The men looked at each other and laughed.

'Mr King has been waitin' for his money. We're authorized to do whatever it takes to get it.'

'Cain't get blood out of a stone,' Jess replied.

Just at that moment the back door opened and Clara entered.

'Where've you been?' Rincorn snapped.

'I don't see that that's any of your business,' she said.

Rincorn's lip turned up in a snarl and, stepping towards her, he seized her by the arm.

'Don't get funny with me, lady,' he snapped.

'Get your hand off me,' she said.

Jess took a step in her direction but before he could take a second the other man reached for his gun and, holding it by the barrel, brought the butt crashing down on the oldster's skull. With a moan he sank to the floor, blood gushing from a gash in the back of his head. Clara cried out and made to help him but a push from Rincorn sent her crashing against the wall. Following up, Rincorn swung his foot and kicked her hard in the stomach and then in the face. Jess was struggling to get up but the second man placed his boot on his back and raked him with his spurs. Jess made one last motion and then lay still as a black tide of unconsciousness overtook him.

'All right,' Rincorn said. 'I think they've got the message.'

Leaning low over the old lady, he hissed in her face:

'We'll be back for the money and next time we won't be so gentle. And by the way, the amount has just doubled. Pay up or this place is gonna burn.'

Spitting on the ground, he moved to go back

through the front room and then, changing his mind, slammed through the back way with his partner following behind.

Clara was struggling to get her breath; her back was aching and she felt sick. After a time she managed to hobble over to where her husband lay, a pool of blood gathering on the carpet.

'Jess,' she pleaded, 'Jess.'

She put her ear next to his mouth. He was still breathing. Battling against her own pain, she managed to stand up straight and get to the sink. Wetting a towel, she went back and began to bathe Jess's head wound. His breathing was laboured and she thought she might be losing him when his eyes opened and he peered up at her.

'Jess, hold on,' she murmured. 'Hold this against your head.'

The flicker of a smile touched his features.

'I been pistol-whipped before,' he said. 'My head hurts and my back sure feels like hell. But what about you?'

She tried to play it down, but when he had heard he was filled with anger.

'Those low-down stinkin' polecats,' he said. 'I ain't gonna let them get away with this.'

He raised himself up a little and then sank back to the floor. His shirt had been ripped apart and there were long cuts and slashes down his back.

'No use in gettin' all worked up,' Clara said. 'First thing, those cuts need cleanin' up. I'll get the iodine.'

She went to a cupboard and came back with the bottle.

'I'm sorry,' she said. 'This is sure gonna hurt.'

'Go ahead,' he mumbled.

Clara was right, but when she had finished he succeeded in sitting up once more.

'I need some of that Tanglefoot,' he said.

Supporting one another they stumbled through to the main room and collapsed on the couch where they lay for some time before Jess suddenly made to stand up.

'Hell,' he said, 'we've plumb forgotten that young lady we left down the cellar.'

He moved towards the door but fell back again.

'I can manage,' Clara said. 'Just you finish that drink and I'll go.'

She was feeling a little better but the punishment she had received had taken a lot out of her. Slowly she made her way back to the stable. It was dark inside and at first she didn't notice anything amiss. Then her heart skipped a beat. The barrel she had moved to cover the ring in the floor had been moved and the stairwell was exposed. With a sudden burst of energy born of desperation she rushed to the hole and shouted down into the darkness.

'Bonny! Bonny! Are you there?'

There was no reply and she called down once again. The only response was the cold air coming up from below. Finally, going backwards so she could cling to the stairs for support, she made her way down. At the bottom she paused for a moment while her eyes adjusted but she soon saw that the place was empty. Only an overturned chair and a couple of extinguished candles told the story of what had happened. Cradling her head in her hands, the old lady began to sob. It was the first time in long years she had been brought so low.

CHAPTER FIVE

Keeping his hat low and his collar high, Kramer stole into town. He had grown a beard during his time in the mountains and felt pretty sure that no one would recognize him. In his pocket he had been carrying a short list of names which Tilly Lush had given him but he had thrown it away on the off chance that if things went wrong and he was discovered, it might spell trouble for those on the list. Once again he kept to the back streets where there were few people about, arriving at the rear of the Bruford house. Coming up to the door, he knocked gently but there was no response. He tried again and if he had looked up he might have seen Jess's face at the window, peering out and trying to make out who it was. After another little time the door was opened slightly to reveal the oldster standing there with a gun in his hand.

'Yeah? What do you want?'

'It's me, Kramer.'

The old man peered closer and then recognized his visitor.

'Kramer!' he said. 'Hell, it's real good to see you. Didn't recognize you with that fur coverin' your face.'

'That was the idea,' Kramer said.

He stepped inside. The old man's features had been in shadow but now Kramer noticed how lined it was. At the same moment Clara entered and he saw immediately her partly closed eye and the bruised swelling beneath it.

'What happened?' Kramer hissed.

'Come on in. Make yourself comfortable. Jess, pour the man a drink.'

She gave Kramer an anxious look.

'It don't matter about us,' she said. 'It's Bonny.'

'We were plannin' to try and make it up the mountain to tell you.'

'There's no way you could have done it,' Kramer said. 'I could barely get down myself.'

He sat down and Jess handed him a glass.

'Where is Bonny?' he said. 'What's been goin' on?'

It didn't take long for the Brufords to explain what had happened. When they had finished Kramer's face was grim.

'I owe you folks an apology,' he said. 'It's my fault you were put at risk.'

'It weren't nothin' to do with you,' Jess said. 'The reason those varmints did this is because they figure we owe them money.'

'Money? What money?'

'King and his boys expect regular payments. We decided we weren't goin' to pay up no more.'

Kramer looked puzzled and then he understood what they were saying.

'Protection money?' he said. 'Things is worse than I even imagined.'

'It's not just us. There's a lot of folks in the same fix. Only we were the ones refused to pay.'

'King is the one who's goin' to pay,' Kramer said.

His emotions were running high; between feeling pity and concern for what had happened to the Brufords and a seething anger at the persons responsible, he didn't know where to start. And he was anxious about Bonny.

'Are you sure you two are OK now?' he said.

'We're fine. It takes more than a beating to put us out of action.'

'Those stinkin' coyotes! How could they do that to a woman, to an old couple like you?'

'Hey, not so much of the old. There's plenty of spit left in us. We'll be fightin' right alongside you when the time comes.'

'It's not us you need to worry about,' Clara said. 'The question is, what do we do about Bonny?'

Over supper Kramer explained what had brought him down from the mountain.

'I've knowed Tilly Lush a long time,' Clara said. 'She's a good woman and she knows what she's talking about. Let me have a look at that list of names.'

'I ain't got it,' Kramer said, 'but I can tell you who they are.'

As he named the people on the list, Clara and Jess

both nodded their heads or uttered little grunts of agreement.

'Yeah, that sounds about right,' Clara said when he had finished.

'And I reckon we could suggest one or two others,' Jess added.

Clara paused.

'I tell you what,' she said. 'Why don't you let us follow up that list of names? We know those folk and it would be a lot easier for us to do it than you.'

'What about King?' Kramer said. 'I don't want to get you or those people into any trouble.'

'It'll be a pleasure to do somethin' in the way of gettin' back at him,' Clara said. 'Besides, I think you've got other matters to deal with.'

Kramer looked at her.

'If you're sure about it,' he said.

'Just you concentrate on getting Bonny back,' Clara said.

'Yeah. That's just what I intend doin'.'

When the meal was finished Kramer got to his feet.

'You goin' already?' Jess said.

'I'll be back but I don't know when,' Kramer replied.

'Just watch your back,' Jess said.

Kramer nodded. Clara got up and he gave her a hug and then went towards the door.

'Ain't you goin' out the back way?' Clara asked.

'Not this time,' Kramer said.

When he had left the Brufords, Kramer turned his

steps towards the centre of town. The sky was dark and there was little activity but ahead of him he could see the lights of the Blue Bucket; Jess had mentioned the reopening of the saloon. Several horses were tied to the hitchrack outside and Kramer stopped to look at them. As he had anticipated, they bore King's brand, a square bisected by a horizontal line – the Bible. Stepping up to the boardwalk, Kramer pushed his way through the batwings. The saloon was quite busy but there was something lacking. The atmosphere was too heavy – there was none of the usual chatter and there were no girls and no piano to enliven the proceedings. A group of four men were lounging at the bar and Kramer guessed they were the owners of the horses. It wasn't difficult – one glance was enough to tell him that these were no ordinary townsfolk but hard men who made their living by the guns they wore slung low. Some of them turned round at his entrance and looked him up and down as he crossed the room. Kramer was in the mood.

'Which one of you is Rincorn?' he said.

It was a gambit, but it worked. One of the men who had his back to Kramer turned slowly round.

'Who's askin?' he said.

'Where's Bonny Lange?'

Rincorn turned to the right and then to the left, looking at his companions with a smirk on his face.

'Any of you boys know somebody called Bonny Lange?'

They grinned and some of them shook their heads

with mock expressions of puzzlement on their faces. Then one of them spoke up.

'Say, isn't she the whore who went missin' a few weeks ago?'

Rincorn turned his leering face to Kramer and shrugged his shoulders.

'I'll ask once more. Where have you taken Bonny Lange?'

Some of the other clients were taking an interest. A few of them knew the girl and either knew or suspected what had happened to her and a few others when King had thrown them out of town. Others were beginning to feel nervous and were looking for the possibilities of shelter.

'Mister,' Rincorn said, 'I don't know who you are but you sure just signed your death warrant.'

There was a slight movement of his hand towards his gun but Kramer's gun was already up and spitting lead. Rincorn reeled backwards, blood spurting from his chest, and a second bullet took him in the throat. One of the other gunslicks had drawn his gun but before he could fire, a bullet from Kramer took him in the stomach and he sank to the floor, groaning. Then Kramer's free hand was fanning the hammer of his Colt Army revolver. Through the haze of smoke he saw one of his two remaining opponents lift from his feet and go crashing against the bar. The other had taken a bullet in the shoulder but succeeded in loosing a shot which tore at Kramer's jacket before another hit sent the gunslick toppling face first to the floor. He slithered forward a few inches and then his body convulsed in its death throes. Kramer dropped to one knee, jamming cartridges into the empty chambers of his gun, but as silence descended it became apparent that the fight was over. Looking about him in case anyone wanted it to continue, Kramer got to his feet and approached the four bodies. Three of them were dead. Kneeling beside the one survivor, the man who had been shot in the stomach, Kramer seized him by the collar. The man screamed but Kramer dragged him to a sitting position.

'Like I said, where's Bonny Lange?' he hissed.

The man eyes sought Kramer's but they were rapidly glazing over.

'Somebody get a doctor!' Kramer shouted, but it was already too late. With a final whimper the man's head dropped back in death. Kramer stood up and turned to the onlookers.

'Anyone lookin' for five hundred dollars' reward?' he asked.

Nobody seemed ready to take up the offer.

'Tell the marshal I ain't runnin', and if anyone gets near King, tell him he's next.'

Gun in hand, Kramer backed towards the exit and clattered through the batwings. Unfastening one of King's horses, he vaulted into leather and set off down the street. He had a kind of rage burning in him now and without thinking he headed in the direction of the Bible. After allowing the horse to have its head till he was well clear of town, he slowed it down to a quick walk in order to save it for what might be needed later. All the same he was fast approaching King's property when he realized that there was a bunch of riders already on his tail and he guessed it was the marshal with a gang of King's hardcases. He also knew there was no way the marshal would take him back to jail. They were out to kill him and they weren't far behind. Veering off the trail, he applied his spurs and set the pinto galloping towards the broken country which lay towards the foothills of the mountains where the snow was lying deep. During the course of his last few weeks in the mountains he had come to know the terrain well and he was able to make reasonable progress where he knew his pursuers would flounder. In particular he knew a treacherous corner where the route narrowed: in good conditions it was an awkward place with crevasses on either side, but now that they were concealed by deep drifts of snow, a slight error of judgement on the part of horse or rider could prove fatal. The pinto was a good mountain horse and knew the dangers even without the careful guidance of its rider. Inch by inch it stepped its way, planting its feet with precision, its ears pricked with concentration. At one point its right foreleg slipped and for a moment it seemed they might plunge into the gulch but then it found firmer ground once more and they were past the narrowest part of the trail. A little further ahead was a pile of rocks, which at some stage had tumbled from higher up the mountain. Once he had reached them Kramer swung down from the pinto and, concealing it behind a couple of the larger boulders, hobbled it. He drew the Sharps from its scabbard and took up a position behind another rock which gave him a clear view back down the trail. Then he waited for a first sign of the riders.

A long time seemed to pass. He was well wrapped for the bitterly cold weather but even so he felt the cold start to bite into his bones. A few flakes of snow began to fall from a leaden sky. He was beginning to think that he had lost the posse or that they had decided to give up and return to town when he caught his first glimpse of the lead rider toiling slowly up the mountainside. It was the marshal and after a few moments another rider appeared. The trail was narrow and they were coming up in single file. There were six of them and from what Kramer could make out, none of them appeared to be regular citizens. There was no mistaking the look of gunmen as they came closer, gradually nearing the danger point. Kramer raised his rifle but held his fire. The marshal's horse was approaching the narrowest part of the path and already seemed to be having difficulty maintaining its balance when its legs seemed to give way and it went belly-deep into the snow. Floundering, the horse began to plunge as the marshal fought desperately to regain control. As if in sympathy, the horse behind began to toss and, losing its footing, went over into the deep snow. The marshal's horse was snorting and whinnying in fear and then suddenly it disappeared from sight. The snow had given way, plunging horse and rider into the deep crevasse beneath. The silence of the mountainside was rent by a hideous scream like the braying of a trumpet; it was impossible to tell whether it was from horse or rider. The second horse was jumping, trying to regain the path, when the rider was flung from his saddle as the horse, too, lost the battle and slid from sight. The horseman sank into snow up to his waist, but Kramer's attention was now concentrated on the rest of the bunch. Seeing what had happened to their comrades, they were trying to turn their horses but it was almost impossible on the narrow, dangerous path. One of the horses reared and at the same moment Kramer squeezed the trigger of the Sharps. The shot rang out across the mountainside and one of the riders fell from his mount under the sharp hoofs of the rearing horse. Kramer fired again, lifting another man out of the saddle and he knew he would have no more to worry about from those two. The remaining riders had succeeded in changing direction. One of them turned and fired but the shot was wild and the bullet smacked into the hillside well away from where Kramer was hiding. Raising the Big Fifty again, he let loose at their retiring figures and one of the horses went down – Kramer couldn't see what had become of the rider. The other horse had disappeared from sight and Kramer knew it was useless to try and stop him. Anyway, he would carry the news to King and that might be no bad thing. Kramer was of the opinion that it did no harm to let your enemy know you were on the warpath.

Getting to his feet, he moved cautiously down the trail, being very careful because he still did not know what had become of the rider of the horse he had shot. He was half expecting a bullet to seek him out, but when he got to the scene he could see that the man was trapped beneath the dead horse, his leg bent where it had got caught in the stirrups and snapped. Kramer ignored his moans and stood over him with the Sharps.

'I'm askin' you what I asked the others. Where's Bonny Lange?'

The man looked up at him, agony written across his features.

'Please,' he begged. 'My leg's busted.'

Kramer drew back the hammer.

'Guess the best thing would be to put you out of your misery right now.'

'Please,' the man groaned.

'Where did they take Bonny Lange?'

The man's eyes were wild with fear and pain.

'She's at King's spread.'

'The Bible?'

'Yeah. Believe me, I had nothin' to do with it.'

Kramer laid the rifle to one side.

'I'm gonna have to pull you from under,' he said, 'and I'll need to get your foot out of the stirrup.'

'Go ahead,' the man muttered.

As carefully as he could, Kramer got the man's foot loose, ignoring his gasps, then tried lifting the horse. It was no use and he considered piling snow under it to try and raise it a little but abandoned the idea as impossible.

'I'll try to do this quick,' he said. 'Are you ready?'

The man nodded and then Kramer, putting his arms under the man's armpits and bracing himself against the snow, heaved as hard as he could. The man's screams rang down the mountain but with a last desperate effort Kramer succeeded in pulling him loose, falling back into the snow as the man's leg came free. Kramer struggled to his feet.

'I got somethin' in my saddle-bags,' he said.

Making his way back to the pinto, he dug out a bottle he had got from a medicine show which contained a mixture of whiskey and morphine and returned to the wounded gunslick.

'Here, take a swallow of this,' he said.

During all the time that had elapsed since he had left the Brufords, Kramer had barely noticed that night had almost descended.

'Ain't nothin' more to be done now,' he said. 'Just do your best to hang on. I'll get a fire goin' and make you as comfortable as I can.'

'You gonna leave me?'

'Like I said, there's nothin' else I can do. When I get down the mountain I'll find a way to spread the word you're up here. Someone'll come to get you.'

The man began to protest but while Kramer set up camp he drifted into unconsciousness, only coming round again later after Kramer had done what he could to set him up. It was late and Kramer needed to move. Bringing the pinto down past the landfall, he climbed into the saddle.

'Just hang on,' he said. 'Keep taking a swallow from that bottle. It won't be long before somebody comes.'

He started to pick his way down the mountain. The clouds had blown over and it was a clear, sharp night. When he reached the foothills dawn had broken but he didn't stop to make breakfast. The man he had left behind needed help badly and although it was somewhat out of his way he headed in the direction of town, keeping his eyes open for any sign of danger. He hadn't gone much further before he saw a lone horseman in the distance coming towards him. He stepped his horse off the trail and, concealed behind some trees, he drew his rifle and awaited the man's arrival. He thought it might be the gunslick who had escaped the shooting or another of King's henchmen but as the figure approached the rising sun glinted off the star on his jacket and he realized it was the deputy marshal, Riff Rogers. He waited till the deputy was almost upon him and then stepped the pinto out from cover.

'Hold it right there!' he snapped.

The marshal didn't seem surprised. Complying with Kramer's command, he drew rein.

'Kramer,' he said. 'Thought I might come across you somewhere.'

'It's a funny time to be ridin' the hills. Guess you

ain't out for an early mornin' constitutional.'

'Why don't you put that rifle down?' Rogers said. 'You might not believe this, but I ain't out to cause you any trouble.'

Kramer considered his words and then with a slight nod of the head he slid the Sharps into its scabbard.

'Start talkin',' he snapped.

'I heard all about what happened yesterday at the Blue Bucket,' Rogers said. 'You were plumb out of order.'

'I had my reasons.'

'Yeah. I also heard about what happened to Bonny Lange. I don't hold with that kind of thing.'

'So where does that put you?' Kramer said.

'There's a few things been goin' on that I don't hold with. I don't believe in strandin' folks in the middle of nowhere; I don't hold with beatin' up old men and women. In fact, there's been quite an accumulation of things and I reckon I finally seen the light.'

'You heard about the Brufords?'

'I've seen what happened to the Brufords.'

'You ride for King and he's the one behind all that.'

'In a way, maybe. But not really. I thought I was representin' law an' order. Now I see I was representin' King's law and order.'

'There's a five hundred dollar reward on my head,' Kramer said. 'You sayin' you got no intention of tryin' to claim on it?'

Rogers laughed.

'Hell, I'd be plumb ashamed if that was the value they put on my head. What did you do, steal some bread from the grocery store?'

'What I did was try to help some of those folks you just referred to. Right now they're lastin' out the winter in a cabin up in the mountains. They're figurin' how they might ever be able to come down again.'

'That was bad,' Rogers replied. 'I felt guilty about it.'

'It was you put in the feed?'

Rogers grunted.

'It weren't an awful lot. I shoulda done more.'

'Your boss McLaren wouldn't have approved.'

'Nope, guess not.'

Mention of McLaren seemed to turn the deputy's thoughts in a new direction.

'What's happened to McLaren?' he said. 'I gather he rode out yesterday with a few of King's boys lookin' for you.'

'He found me,' Kramer said.

Rogers looked at him closely.

'He ain't comin' back down the mountain,' Kramer continued. 'Neither are a few of the others. Are you still sure you ain't gonna put me under arrest?'

Rogers didn't reply for a moment.

'Like I say,' he concluded. 'I reckon I seen the

light. McLaren was askin' for it.'

'There's one up there bad hurt with a broken leg. He needs help quick.'

'And you want me to see to it? What about you, Kramer? What are you intendin' to do?'

'I got business with King,' Kramer replied.

'You aimin' to ride clear on to the Bible? You'll never make it.'

The deputy marshal stopped and looked at Kramer's firm set features.

'I guess King's boys made a bad mistake when they took Bonny Lange,' he said.

'You see to that *hombre* up the mountain,' Kramer replied. 'When I've finished with King I'll see you back in town.'

'There's still that price on your head. You sure like takin' risks.'

'You're the marshal now,' Kramer said.

Touching his spurs to the pinto's flanks he edged past Rogers and then turned from the trail leading to town in the direction of the Bible.

When Rincorn had returned to the Bible with Bonny Lange, Zebulon King wasn't too sure how he felt about it. On the one hand he didn't like the idea of anyone escaping his justice; it set a bad precedent and whoever did so had to be made an example of. On the other hand, it was something he could have done without at this particular juncture and he felt uncomfortable about having the former saloon girl there at all. He was in a bit of a quandary wondering what to do with her and for the time being arranged to have her locked in an empty barn. He had to admit that she didn't look like a girl from the erstwhile Golden Garter. When Rincorn had ridden off, he began to feel restless. Rincorn had said he had found the girl hiding in a cellar of the livery stables. What was she doing there? Had she somehow found her own way back to Kingsville after being exiled with the rest of them? It didn't seem likely. In the end he got to his feet and made his way to the barn. Lifting aside the heavy wooden bar which secured the door, he went inside. The girl was lying on top of some hay and when he entered she got to her feet. If King had expected her to be scared he was mistaken. She was shook up by what had happened but something had snapped inside her. Coming on top of her experiences on the mountain it had hardened her to King and his ways.

'How dare you allow your men to drag me here?' she said. 'I demand to be released.'

'Never mind that,' King replied. 'I thought I'd got rid of you and your kind. What were you doing back in Kingsville?'

'What right did you have to expel us?' she said. 'Just who do you think you are?'

'I know what type you are,' King responded. 'Yes, and the rest of you. Whores and gamblers, no-goods and drunks. None of you fit to live in civilized company.'

He took a step towards her and then another but

she did not flinch. She had struck a defiant attitude; her head was erect, her cheeks were flaming and her eyes flashing. Suddenly King felt a prick of desire. If she had been dressed in her gaudy fineries he might have been repelled. If she had adopted a different attitude she might not have had the effect on him that she was having. But looking like she did, looking so young and yet so womanly, her long hair falling to her shoulders, he felt a sting of desire such as he had not felt in a long time, if he had felt it at all. Fighting back his feelings, he tried to return to the issue at hand.

'I'll ask you once more, how did you get back to Kingsville? Are the rest of them hiding out somewhere in town? If they are I won't show any leniency this time. Your punishment won't be banishment; it will be something a lot worse.'

'I'm not scared of you or your threats,' she responded. 'Used to be you held the town in the palm of your hand but that's all changing. People have got wise to you. You'll see.'

King was not used to being defied. Coupled with his rising lust was a growing anger not unmixed with a vague sense of disquiet. Things had not been going right of late. He felt a little off kilter. Maybe she had a point.

'Listen to me, you little whore,' he said. 'I want to know right now what you were doing in Kingsville and you'd better tell me.'

'And if I don't? What are you going to do about it?'

He was close to her now. He could smell her perfume and feel the warmth of her quivering body. She was like a ripe fruit; she was Eve and Jezebel and Delilah and all those temptresses he had read about rolled into one. Part of him was trying to fight against the urge he felt to possess her and another was telling him to make her pay for everything she and her kind had done to bring strong men down, men like himself who stood for decency and sobriety. For a moment he stood immobile, his face working in a spasm of indecision and desire, and then he lurched forward, grabbing her by the shoulder and pulling at her dress.

'What are you doing?' she screamed. 'Have you taken leave of your senses?'

She struggled against him as he tore her dress asunder, exposing the firm lift of her breasts. His hand was reaching down but then she brought her knee up and he felt a wave of pain engulf him. He bent double and she broke free of his grip. She ran to the far end of the barn and then he was after her again, flinging himself on top of her. They went down together in the hay; forcing her down and fighting against her writhing frame he succeeded in straddling her. Pressing her arms down with a firm grip, he lowered his head, seeking her lips, but she wasn't finished yet. With a howl he reeled back, blood pouring from his face where she had bitten him. As he did so she renewed her struggles to free herself, fighting with a strength she had not known she possessed. She was like a wildcat, spitting into his face as she managed to free one of her hands with which she clawed him across the cheek. Instinctively he reached up to feel the wound and she rolled him over, struggling desperately to regain her feet. He reached after her and pulled her back and then suddenly all desire drained out of him. Standing aside he let out a huge groan and covered his head with his hands before turning and staggering towards the barn door. His mind was racing. He had succumbed to temptation. The Devil was in that barn and he had to get away, even while he knew there was nowhere for him to run to. Wherever he went he was tainted, he was marked by a flaming brand and banished now from the world of righteousness and decency. Staggering through the door, he had just enough presence of mind left to slam it behind him and drop the bar which would keep the wickedness and lure of the temptress contained within. Like someone driven by demons, he lurched into the house and for the first time in a long while sought for refuge in a bottle of brandy he thought he had eschewed. Back in the barn Bonny flung herself at the barn door in an effort to break it open but it was no use She looked about her, trying to stay rational, but then sank to the floor sobbing and crying, holding the ripped shreds of her dress about her.

After leaving the deputy, Kramer rode at a steady pace in the direction of King's spread, the Bible. The burning rage he had felt the previous day had been replaced by a cold and intense calm and he felt clear-headed, alert and decisive. He had a clean new-washed feeling like he had stepped out of an icy mountain stream. He knew for certain now that Bonny Lange was being held at King's ranch. He gritted his teeth and set his mind against thinking what might have happened to her. It wasn't altogether clear where King's range lands began. At certain points on the perimeter there were signs and a section had recently been fenced, but it was an indication of King's overweening ego that he did not feel the necessity to demarcate his property clearly. He was the old time baron. The whole area belonged to him and who was going to question where his domain legally began and ended? Kramer guessed he was on Bible territory when he began to come on groups of cattle, their tails turned to the wind, drifting idly across the snowy landscape. They were looking gaunt; icicles hung from their eyes and ears and their legs were bleeding from walking in crusted snow. Here and there lay the frozen bodies of cattle that had not made it. Kramer wondered why more effort had not been made to see to their wellbeing but guessed that though he owned a big spread, cattle business was not one of King's primary concerns. Again it was typical of his ego to want to be the boss of the biggest ranch in the territory; it was all part of the show. Kramer was expecting to see the odd cowboy out working the range but there was no sign of anybody. He continued on his way until, topping a slight rise in the ground, he saw the ranch-house ahead of him. Drawing to a halt, he got out his field glasses and swept the area. A thin spiral of smoke ascended from the ranch-house but apart from that there was no sign of anyone, no movement. Behind the ranch-house stood the bunkhouse and beyond that several barns and stables. There were horses in the corrals. He kept the glasses trained on the buildings, bringing them down so he could survey the ground. The snow in the yard was churned up by horses' hoofs and there were footprints in the snow leading to the larger of the barns. The rest of the snow was comparatively unsoiled. Slipping the glasses back into their holder, he continued to sit the pinto, trying to interpret what he had seen. It seemed that the likeliest place to find Bonny was the barn. She might be in the ranch-house but those footprints suggested otherwise. In any case, it was a good place to start. It would be comparatively easy to make his way to the barn to investigate. If she wasn't there he could turn to the ranch-house.

Touching his spurs to the pinto's flanks, he moved on, aiming to get as close to the ranch-house as he could without being detected. There was a line of trees leading towards the corrals, passing by the side of the ranch-house, and he rode into them before alighting and tying the horse. He reached for the Sharps and then, changing his mind about taking it, checked his Colts. Then he cautiously began to make his way through the trees. He expected King to have the approaches to the ranch-house guarded but he was heartened by what he had seen. Daylight was fading and the trees provided good cover but he was still careful in case any of King's men were concealed among them.

Proceeding this way, he had almost come alongside the ranch-house when the door was flung open and a man emerged carrying a blazing torch of wood. Instinctively Kramer pressed himself against the nearest tree bole. He had never met Zebulon King but from the descriptions he had been given there was no mistaking that it was him. King stopped for a moment on the veranda before stomping on and Kramer could see that he was in an extremely agitated frame of mind. Reaching the end of the veranda, he disappeared round the corner but the burning torch indicated his passage. He was moving quickly in the direction of the barn.

For a moment, taken aback by these developments, Kramer stood confused, not sure what to make of what he had seen. Then his faculties resumed their normal workings and, realizing that King was clearly bent on some nefarious purpose, it dawned that he was about to set fire to the barn. Kramer had been working on the theory that Bonny Lange was being held there. Whatever was happening seemed only to confirm this supposition. Suddenly he realized the full import of the situation and plunged forwards, little reckoning whether anyone saw him or not, intent only on reaching the barn as quickly as he could. At the same instant smoke began to emerge from the direction of the barn and then a snake-like column of flame climbed above its roof. Running as hard as he could but hampered by the snow, Kramer emerged into the open space in front of the barn. There was no sign of King but a trail left in the snow led round the side of the barn in the direction of the corrals. Kramer noted it almost mechanically because his attention was centred solely on the barn. The fire had already caught a firm hold and flames were shooting from the sides and the roof. A thick pall of smoke billowed into the air filled with sparks and ash. Pulling his bandanna up around his mouth, Kramer pulled at the strong wooden bar which held the door shut but he couldn't open it. Again he struggled to try and raise it but for some reason it would not move. Perhaps the fire had warped the doorframe or King had done something to render it immovable. Standing back, Kramer shouted Bonny's name.

'Bonny! Bonny! Are you in there?'

There was no reply and he tried once more, again without success. The smoke was dense now and he was coughing and spluttering. Growing increasingly desperate, he looked about for some means of gaining access to the building but there seemed to be none. As quickly as he could he ran round the side to the back where there was a doorway high up with a pulley system which was obviously used to hoist loads to the top. Flames were already licking at it and the chain might become too hot to hold. There was no guarantee either that the door would allow access to the blazing barn but it was the only possible chance he had. Seizing the chain, he wrapped his legs round it and began to haul himself up. The whole area around was illuminated by the lurid flickering glow of the fire and instinctively he looked about expecting some of Kramer's men to be on their way to help douse the flames but there was still no sign of anyone. It was peculiar. Obviously King felt himself entirely secure in his fortress and enjoyed privacy. All the same, it was odd. It was one less thing for him to worry about.

He was well on the way to the top when a branch of fire shot out from the wall above his head. Desperately he renewed his efforts, trying to get above that point before the metal became too hot to handle. He glanced down. It seemed a long way to the ground. He was almost level with the flame and the chain was hot in his hands. He braced himself for the part he must negotiate through the fire and then pulled hard on the chain. Like some strange phoenix he was embraced by the flames but his thick clothing offered some protection. His bandanna covered most of his face but he felt his eyebrows singeing. His hands were burning with the heat of the metal. Pulling hard hand over hand, he made a big effort and heaved his body clear of the flames, which now raged about his legs. His clothing was smouldering and he could barely hold on to the chain. He grimaced in an effort to bear the searing pain across the palms of his hands, forcing himself to continue despite the burning. He was just below the level of the door and he reached with his leg for the narrow platform on to which it opened. He kicked hard but it seemed he was too far out. He kicked at the wall of the barn and succeeded in pushing himself away from the wall. Once he had gained a little momentum he began to move his legs so that the chain swung and as he made a final effort to pull himself another inch or two higher his foot found the edge of the platform. The chain swung back and his foot slipped off but on the next swing he managed to push it further into the aperture and press his boot down so that his foot remained in place, slowing the swing of the chain. He tried to get his knee on to the platform but it slipped off when the chain swung. There was only one chance, and that was to launch himself towards the platform when the chain swung closest to it. Gasping with the strain of clinging to the hot metal he prepared himself to let go the next time it approached the wall of the barn. There was still a gap but he knew he must risk everything on one attempt to gain the platform. If he succeeded he would gain his perch; if he failed he would plummet like a stone back to the earth. The chain reached the outermost reach of its parabola and as it swung back he launched himself forward, letting go of the red-hot chain as he did so. His knees struck the edge of the wooden platform and for a moment he had a sickening feeling that he was about to fall backwards. Leaning forwards and fighting to gain some sort of purchase, he tottered for a moment before regaining his equilibrium and pitching forward in an untidy heap against the door over which the winch was suspended. He hit it head first and could have badly injured his skull except that the door gave way and opened inwards, sending him crashing to the floor inside the barn.

In an instant he was on his feet and taking account of the situation. He was in the barn loft and at the opposite end, beside a pile of hay, was a trapdoor. He ran forward and peered down but could see little because of the thick blanket of smoke which shrouded the floor below. He looked for a ladder but there was none. He would have to jump into the heart of the furnace. Sitting on the edge, he lowered himself as far as he could and then let go. He hit the ground below with a thud, rolling forward to try and cushion the shock. The heat was intense and roaring, rearing flames cut off the back of the barn. Keeping low, he struggled forward, searching desperately for Bonny. Then, just when it seemed he was wrong about her being there, he saw her lying beside the door. Coughing and gasping, his lungs seared by the heat, he bent down and picked her up. She did not move and he had no time to tell whether she was dead or injured. The only thing now was to get out of that inferno, but there was no way he could get back up to the loft. In desperation he began to kick at the barn door, but it was solid and did not give way a fraction. He couldn't last much longer; the flames were devouring the whole of the barn. The heat was unbearable and his lungs were almost refusing to function any longer. He sank to his knees, still holding the girl, having to admit defeat, when suddenly with a tremendous explosion of noise, one entire wall of the barn collapsed, sending flames soaring high into the night sky where sparks flew about like fireflies. The cold wintry air blew into the open barn, battling with the acrid smoke, and Kramer took a deep rasping breath before struggling upright and beginning to make his way through the smoke and flames towards the open air. His eyes stung and he could barely see his way through the dense billowing clouds of black smoke but he drove forwards, staggering and stumbling, towards the outside world. A beam came down with a crash just in front of him and then there was a sound like a loud groan and another wall of the barn slumped inwards. He realized that the whole structure was about to topple but it didn't matter now because he was through the gap and stumbling away from the barn. He wasn't aware of where he was but he could hear the braying and snorting of the panic-stricken horses in the corral before his feet gave way beneath him and he tumbled to the ground, carrying Bonny with him.

In a moment he had recovered and, putting his ear to the girl's mouth, listened for sounds of breathing. It was erratic but it was there. She was covered in black ash and he couldn't tell if she had been affected by the fire in any other way. He began to brush the ash from her and then, not knowing whether he was doing the right thing, he began to rub snow across her face.

'Bonny, he whispered. 'Bonny, it's me, Kramer.'

He continued his ministrations, talking to her, becoming increasingly desperate as she failed to respond.

'Bonny, can you hear me? Please, breathe. Please come round.'

He held her close to him. All around the night-time scene was lit up by the fire and there was a loud roar and crackle as the flames continued to devour what was left of the barn. Bonny and he seemed to be the only people around but it didn't register with him. He could only think about Bonny and was giving up hope that she would survive when her eyelids suddenly opened and she looked up at him with pain and bewilderment in her eyes.

'It's all right,' he said. 'It's me, Kramer. Everything will be all right.'

A dawning light of understanding touched her blackened features.

'Kramer!' she gasped. 'Where am I? What happened?'

She sat up and looked about her.

'There was a fire,' Kramer said, 'but I reached you in time.'

Now that she was fully conscious the memory of

what had happened to her began to return and she shivered.

'We need to get out of here,' Kramer said.

Without attempting further explanation, Kramer got to his feet and, picking her up once more, began to move away. When he got to the trees he made his way to where he had left the pinto, the fire now a fading glow seen through the intervening tree trunks.

'Can you ride?' he asked.

Bonny nodded her head and he hoisted her up. Now that they were away from the fire and relatively safe, for the first time he became conscious of his own injuries. He was burned and singed in various places but the most serious damage was to his hands which were badly burned from the hot metal chain up which he had climbed. Across his palms were lurid welts; he plunged them into the snow before climbing into the saddle but it hurt even to hold the reins. It didn't matter. Battered and bruised she might be, but Bonny was alive. She was with him, they were together again and this time he wasn't going to let her fall into anyone's clutches. Thinking that way, he turned the pinto in the direction of Kingsville.

CHAPTER SIX

Back at the cabin on the mountains, Reynard Armitage, working to clear away some of the snow in the immediate vicinity, was taken by surprise when he looked up to see Deputy Marshal Rogers approaching. His first thought was that King had found out where they were hiding and sent Rogers to complete the business he had started by banishing them. He made to get his derringer then remembered he had left it in his jacket pocket in the cabin. As the deputy approached, Armitage saw that he was carrying something across the chestnut's back. Further reaction was halted as the deputy perceived him and called out.

'I've just left Kramer. He said you were hidin' away somewhere up here.'

Armitage did not reply.

'I have a wounded man with me.'

The deputy came up alongside the gambler and swung down from his horse.

'Give me a hand to get him indoors,' he said, and seeing that Armitage still hesitated, he added:

'Don't worry. I come in friendship. I'll explain everything once we've got this *hombre* inside.'

Before anything else could be said the cabin door opened and Tilly Lush appeared with the two girls.

'Hello!' Rogers said. 'I guess you didn't expect to see me.'

With Armitage's assistance he carried the wounded man inside the cabin.

'Put him on the bed,' Tilly said. The man moaned slightly as they did so but he appeared to be only semi-conscious.

'Who is he?' Tilly asked.

'One of King's men. He was ridin' with a posse on Kramer's tail.'

Tilly looked anxious.

'I reckon I don't need to say who got the better of the encounter,' the deputy said.

When they had made the man as comfortable as they could, Rogers outlined what had happened since Kramer had left them.

'You say Kramer's gone off to find Bonny,' Tilly remarked when he had concluded. 'Surely he'll be playin' straight into King's hands. He'll never get in and out of the Bible with King's men lookin' out for him.'

'Yeah, I guess it looks bad. But it ain't as bad as it seems.'

'How's that?' Armitage said.

'Because he's gonna find that ranch pretty much deserted. Most of King's owlhoots have taken up residence in Kingsville just lately. That's one reason why Kramer caught up with some of them at the Blue Bucket and why McLaren was able to get a few of them together and set off in pursuit so quickly. I ain't too sure just what's goin' on, but I reckon there's somethin' afoot.'

'Then hadn't you better be gettin' back there?' Tilly said. 'You can find a way down even if we can't.'

'That's the main reason I come on this far,' Rogers said. 'There's no cause for any of you to stay up here much longer. The snow's beginnin' to thaw lower down and there's a way through. It ain't too easy but it can be managed.'

'The girls ain't in no fit state to be climbin' about these mountains, thaw or no thaw.'

'Nope, I didn't expect they would be. What I'm proposin' is that you remain here for the moment and see what you can do for that injured varmint – he's certainly in no position to cause any trouble.'

'You sure about that?'

'You seen the state he's in. That leg is plumb busted. He'll be doin' well just to pull through at all.'

'And what then?' Tilly said.

'Like I say, somethin's brewin' in town. Once I get back I'll make arrangements for you all to be brought down. Whatever happens I don't think you have anythin' to worry about now that McLaren's gone. There's a lot of folks comin' out now and startin' to face up to King. Hell, I'm one of 'em.'

Tilly seemed to think over what the deputy had said.

'Seems like the only real thing to be done,' she concluded.

She turned to Armitage.

'Why don't you head back with Deputy Rogers? If things are buildin' to a showdown, he might need every man he can get.'

Armitage had put on his jacket and now smoothed its creases.

'Your suggestion has much to recommend it,' he said. 'Excepting that it would be leaving you ladies without support in what can only still be termed somewhat dire circumstances.'

'I can look after things here. And from what the deputy has said, it won't be for too much longer.'

Armitage turned to the deputy.

'I think we would both value your considered opinion in this matter,' he said.

The deputy raised his brows.

'It's up to you, Armitage. I reckon Miss Lush will be fine for a few more days, but I understand your concern.'

Armitage smiled.

'I sure hate to leave you, Miss Lush,' he said, 'but if Mr Rogers is of the opinion that things may be coming to a head in Kingsville, I feel it behoves me to be there when it comes to pass.'

He thought for a moment.

'I would draw your attention to the fact that I am not in possession of a horse.'

Rogers laughed.

'It might not be too comfortable, but that chestnut can manage two – at least most of the way.'

'Then the matter is resolved,' Armitage said.

The deputy walked through to the bedroom and came back with a pair of Colts.

'The owlhoot's,' he said. 'Strap 'em on. You're gonna need more than that there derringer if it comes to real shootin'.'

When Zebulon King looked back to see the barn burning, he felt a huge wave of relief come rolling over him. Those flames he saw were the flames of hell, destroying the temptress who had tried to beguile him from the paths of righteousness. They were the wrath that devours the ungodly and more than ever he had become the heavens' instrument. He had become the angel of vengeance. As he sat on his horse and witnessed the barn come crashing down the awareness began to grow in him that this was only the beginning. He felt a surging realization of his appointed role in bringing destruction to the ungodly. He had tried to banish the evildoers from the habitations of men but it had proved fruitless; the wicked were too far gone in their sins. Surely the time had come to tear out the canker of ungodliness by the root. What he had done on a small scale to the barn and its occupant must be repeated. The whole town of Dirt Crossing was condemned to destruction and he was ordained to carry out the sentence. He had tried to sanctify it by giving it his own name, but the town had proved unworthy of the honour he had given it. It must revert to its own name, its unsanctified name. The people had never accepted his yoke or bowed their heads to his decrees. They were accursed and must be removed from the pastures of righteousness. Only by doing that could he ensure that the railroad companies would accede to his demands, only by doing so could he ensure the continued growth of his own empire of the godly. And the evil had even spread to his own followers. He had seen dissension grow under his very roof. He must winnow the crop, fan the chaff from the grain. He had made a beginning: now it was incumbent that he see through what he had started.

For a few days after Kramer arrived back at the Brufords with Bonny the town was quiet but there was an air of brooding menace hanging over it. It was like the quiet before a storm with electricity flickering on the horizon. People's nerves were on edge. They didn't know just what to expect but something was about to happen. The Brufords themselves were making a good recovery from their ordeal and they at least were experiencing a reduction of tension. Kramer explained to them what had happened since he walked out of their door. With the demise of the marshal and Rincorn, a load was lifted from their backs. They no longer feared the arrival of any of

King's men and they made little effort to conceal the girl. Under Clara's ministrations she too made a quick recovery and the presence of Kramer was an additional help. She and Kramer were reticent about the feelings they had for one another but Clara's perspicacious eye was quick to read the signs.

'Dang me,' she remarked to Jess. 'I reckon that there fire weren't the only way those two got scorched.'

On the third day after his return Kramer received a call from the deputy marshal. Somehow, although Kramer had not said anything to anybody apart from the Brufords, word had got out about the burning of the barn.

'I figured maybe you had somethin' to do with it,' Rogers said.

'In a way,' Kramer replied, 'but it weren't my doing.'

In a few clipped sentences he outlined what had happened when he reached the Bible.

'Hell,' Rogers said. 'Looks like King has really flipped.'

'I wonder what's become of him,' Jess said. 'So far as I know, he ain't been seen around town.'

'How are you all fixed later?' the deputy said.

'What do you mean?'

'There's few folk I'd like Kramer to meet.'

Jess turned to Clara.

'I guess you puttin' the word round is beginnin' to have an effect,' he said.

'I don't want to impose on you folks,' Rogers said. 'You'll know these people but Kramer won't. I was just thinkin' it might be a good time to sit down and decide what we're goin' to do about King. Seems like I'm not the only one to have come to his senses.'

'We'd be right proud to see you all,' Clara said. 'Why don't you call by this evenin' and have somethin' to eat. We can all get together and talk afterwards.'

That's mighty good of you,' Rogers replied. 'There'll be a few of us, maybe about seven or eight. Hope that's OK.'

'It's fine.'

The deputy left and the day passed. Clara went to work in the kitchen, assisted by Bonny. Kramer and Jess took a walk. A lot of noise was coming from the Blue Bucket and Kramer was tempted to take a look inside.

'I don't like it,' Jess cautioned. 'There's somethin' not right about things. I wouldn't mind a drink myself but it might not be wise to get caught up in anythin' just at the moment.'

'You're right,' Kramer replied. 'Especially with this meeting arranged for tonight.'

'I reckon I can tell you who'll be there,' Bruford responded. 'Clara's been soundin' out folks. I'm pretty sure Clint Sager will be one of 'em. He runs the saddle shop. Jay Smith will probably bring along his oldest boy. They do all kinds of odd jobs around town, buildin' and repairs and such like. Ray Holder, he's another, and old Doc Cale. None of 'em are what you would call fighting men – neither am I – but we've been pushed around just once too often. I guess it needed someone like you to make us wake up to what has to be done.'

'If it really does come to a showdown, it might not be pretty. King has a lot of hard-cases ridin' for him. He won't give up easily.'

'Yeah, I think we realize that. But never mind us; how about you? We got a real stake in this town. You're a stranger with no ties. You didn't need to get involved in any of this.'

'I was a stranger,' Kramer replied. 'But I sure got a stake now.'

The oldster looked up into his face.

'I think I got you,' he said. 'You referrin' to Miss Bonny?'

Kramer looked slightly shamefaced.

'Clara figured there might be something between you,' Jess added.

'She's right,' Kramer replied.

'Well, time comes for a man to throw his loop over a filly. At least, he thinks that's how it is till he finds he's the one who's been harness broke.'

'That's the way it was with you and Clara?' Kramer commented.

'Sure. But since she slipped that nosebag on I been like a grain-fed horse. Wouldn't have gone back to the old arrangement.'

'I'll take that as a recommendation,' Kramer replied.

Jess Bruford's predictions were proved correct that evening when the group assembled. There were eight newcomers. The room was a little crowded and there were some difficulties about accommodating them all, but with some of them sitting on the stairs or the floor or leaning against a wall, they just about managed. Clara had set out a number of dishes on the table and there was strong coffee to go with them. Kramer was introduced to them all. They seemed a good bunch but he had reservations about how they would cope if and when it came to the push. They were looking towards him and the deputy for leadership and when they had eaten there was an air of expectancy.

'I want to say a few words to you all,' Rogers said. 'But I'm waitin' for one more arrival.'

He looked out the window.

'Ah, here he comes now.'

A few minutes later the door was thrown open and Kramer's face creased in a smile when he recognized Reynard Armitage.

'I would have brought him along earlier,' Rogers grinned, 'but it seemed he had a little business to attend to at the Blue Bucket.'

Armitage seemed as pleased to see Kramer as Kramer was in seeing him. Most of the others were familiar with the gambler. Some of them had even lost money to him but somehow they didn't resent it; the general opinion was that he had won fair and square. They might not altogether approve of his profession but there was something about the man which made them warm to him.

'You must excuse my delay,' he announced. 'I was pleased to observe that the old Golden Garter has been resurrected in the guise of the Blue Bucket. I felt it incumbent upon me to re-introduce myself and resume something of our erstwhile relationship.'

'How much did you win?' Kramer asked.

'I was persuaded to participate in a game of draw poker, despite the unprepossessing appearance of some of the players, and am pleased to be able to say that I emerged from that particular establishment rather more solvent than when I went in.'

Armitage took his place and Rogers prepared to have his say.

'As you folks all know, I used to be deputy marshal to McLaren. Guess I still am deputy marshal – leastways nobody's asked me to hand in my badge. Like a lot of the townsfolk, I was fooled into believin' Zebulon King was good for this town. Sure, he helped put it on the map; he built it up, provided some basic law and order, spruced things up and seemed to have clamped down on some of the rowdiness. But then he began to go too far. It was when he exiled Mr Armitage and his colleagues that I finally came to the conclusion that something needed to be done to stop him. Power seemed to have gone to his head and without our really being aware of it, he had taken over completely.'

'And that ain't all,' Clint Sager interjected. 'We all

know how King started to take some pretty mean *hombres* into his employ. It was about that time they started to demand money from us, protection money. I don't know how much that was King's doing or if somehow things got out of his control. Maybe it was some of his boys takin' matters into their own hands. Either way, it made no difference: we still had to start payin' up.'

'Some of his boys could get mighty rough,' the doctor said. 'I can't say how many times I've been called out lately but it sure has grown.'

'I think we're all agreed about how things have been lately,' Sager commented. 'None of us want trouble but it seems to me we've been driven into a corner and now we got no choice.'

It was Ray Holder who raised the first doubtful note.

'King ain't the sort to listen to reason,' he said. 'He's got experienced gunfighters on his payroll. How many of us are there? I mean, apart from the few we got here? What sort of a chance do we have?'

There were a few mumbles and one or two people nodded in agreement as the deputy stepped forward again.

'There are a few more I reckon we can count on. Something else might be in our favour too – I think Clint kinda touched on it. It's my belief that King is not going to be able to count on the support of all of his boys. Some of 'em have ambitions to take over the Bible. Some of 'em just don't like the way he's been doin' things. That's why he had to re-open the Blue Bucket.'

'And grateful to him I am for that,' Armitage interrupted, fingering a roll of notes he kept in the inside pocket of his black coat. Rogers' words seemed to stem the first signs of unease in the company, but one or two of the men looked uncomfortable. Kramer glanced at Clara Bruford. She seemed to be stifling something down. Suddenly she began to speak in an impassioned tone.

'Jess and me, we're just recoverin' from a beating we took at the hands of some of King's men. Not only that, but they took Miss Bonny away with them and if it hadn't have been for Mr Kramer, I don't know what might have happened to her. The fact of the matter is that King and his men are out of control. If they can do that to a couple of old folks and a young girl, who's to say what they might not stoop to next? We just ain't got a choice. We either stand up to King now or we're lost. This might be our only chance to do somethin' about the situation. And speaking personally, I'd rather make a stand, even if we lose, than just give up and take whatever King decides to dish out.'

Her words appeared to have a rallying effect and Kramer, taking his cue, stepped forward.

'Clara's right,' he said. 'I'm new to this place but I can see what's been happenin'. I've seen similar things in other places and believe me, you ain't got a choice. The only chance you have of living a decent civilized life is by facing up to King. OK, you might lose, but if you don't face up to him you've lost anyhow. In my experience, and like I say I've been around and seen situations like this before, victory lies with the brave, the courageous, the plain simple folk who are workin' to build a decent life for themselves and their families. What are any of us doin' out here? There's an easier life to be had back east, but this is where we've chosen to carve out a good life in freedom, with our own bones and sinews, our own hard graft and intelligence, our own dreams. Are any of you willin' to give that all up now and bow down to a tyrant and a bunch of no-good spoilers? No-one wants trouble, no one looks for a fight. But when there's no option but to fight for what you believe, then you have to step forward and be counted. That's what you've done by comin' here tonight and I'm proud to stand alongside you folk.'

For a few moments after he had finished there was silence and then Clara began to clap. Someone else joined in and then another person cheered. Rogers stepped out again.

'Kramer has spoken for us all,' he said. 'It's not just him you're applauding but yourselves.'

'What do we do next?' a voice called.

The noise quieted down. A new air of determination had taken over.

'That really depends on King,' Rogers said. 'What we need to do is be prepared. I know you can all handle a gun but you might not have used one for a while. Check them over. Make sure they're to hand if and when you need them. Kramer and I will take the lead but be ready to back us up.'

He turned to Kramer.

'Have you anything to add?'

Kramer pondered for a moment.

'King is actin' erratically,' he said. 'I reckon we've all got the feelin' that somethin's about to blow. Be ready when it happens. Be ready to come to each other's support real quick. Any one of you might have a visit from King's gunslicks. Some of 'em are runnin' wild. There's no knowin' what they might try.'

As the meeting drew to a close and people began to leave, Armitage turned to Kramer.

'Well, I wonder which way the deck is stacked?' he remarked. 'Let's hope we can show King a hand of five all carrying the same complexion when he draws the cards.'

After riding away from the blazing barn, Zebulon King made his way to town where he put up incognito at the Alhambra hotel. He owned the place and kept a suite of rooms for just such an occasion as this. Some of the staff might have recognized him but they were under strict instructions to keep his whereabouts a secret. Normally he would have kept Rincorn on hand as his go-between but he had heard nothing of him for a few days. Instead he sent a message to another of his gunslicks, a man by the name of Wheeler, to come to him at the Alhambra. When he arrived Wheeler had more bad news to tell. A lot of the men were spending time at the Blue Bucket and there was growing dissension.

'I reckon you need to do somethin',' he said.

'What the boys do at the Blue Bucket does not concern me.'

'It should. Weed out a couple of the ringleaders now and it might save you a heap of trouble later.'

'Like I say, I'm not interested. See to it yourself if you like but right now I got somethin' else I want you to do.'

'Yeah? What's that?'

'Dynamite,' King said.

'Dynamite?'

'I need a heap of the stuff. You know where to find it.'

Wheeler's face relaxed into a big grin.

'Now you're talkin',' he said. 'I knowed you wouldn't just sit by and watch things go down the pan. I figured you had somethin' in mind all along.'

King gave him a weary glance.

'That's right,' he said. 'I sure have.'

Despite King's words, Wheeler left still feeling puzzled by his employer's state of mind. King didn't look good. For the first time Wheeler began to wonder whether he was backing the right horse. He would just have to keep his ear to the ground and jump whichever way was necessary when the time came. In the meantime he had a job to do. When he had gone King threw himself on the bed and reached for a glass standing on the table. Once he had moved in, he kept to his rooms, having his food delivered to him. He also kept in stock some bottles of good wine and rye. He made no pretence now of renouncing alcohol. Alone in his luxurious apartment, he drank hard and waited for the call of heaven which would bid him carry out the task allotted to him, the task of cleansing the town of unrighteousness, of applying to it the burning brand. That was all that mattered now. Finally the summons came.

Deputy Marshal Rogers had been weighing up the situation. The brooding, sinister atmosphere that hung over town had grown heavier. He looked out the window of his office at the Blue Bucket from which there issued a lot of noise. Despite King's sanctions, somebody had imported a piano and its tinkling strains rang down the deserted street, accompanied by riotous voices singing in disharmony. There were sounds of laughter and occasionally a loud shout. The place had been more or less taken over by King's men; they were getting increasingly rowdy and trouble was in the offing. Thinking hard, Rogers came to a conclusion. He was getting tired of waiting on King to make the next move. The men who had attended the meeting at the Bruford house were likely to be getting nervous. It wasn't doing their morale any good to be kept waiting indefinitely. Maybe the time had come to make a move, to force King's hand. Strapping on his gun belt, he opened the door, stepped into the street and started walking slowly towards the Blue Bucket. It was evening and the sun had just dropped behind the mountains. Dirty snow lay heaped against the boardwalks and there were icy patches which crunched beneath his boots. A cold wind blew and the horses tied at the hitchrack looked about them with uneasy eyes and stamped their feet. Rogers glanced about him as he walked but apart from the noise emanating from the saloon there were no signs of life. The place was like a ghost town where all the sounds of previous existence had been gathered into one roaring place which suddenly became even louder. As he approached a shot rang out and then another. There was a shattering of glass followed by laughter and then a lull before the noise resumed, slightly more muted. The piano, briefly quieted, began to play again. Rogers slammed through the batwings, taking in the scene at a glance. A couple of men were standing with their guns still smoking. The mirror behind the bar was shattered into fragments.

'You boys havin' fun?' Rogers remarked.

A hush descended, broken by a few stray notes of the piano before the piano player stopped, swivelling round to see what was happening behind him.

'It weren't nothin', Deputy,' somebody said. 'The boys were just lettin' off some steam.'

Rogers approached the two owlhoots.

'Sidearms ain't allowed,' he said. 'Put 'em away

and then drop your gun belts to the floor. And make it real slow.'

Both men hesitated. For a moment the issue hung in the balance. Then one of them swung his six-gun up. In the same instant Rogers's gun was in his hand and spitting lead. The man reeled back, clutching his arm as the Colt spun from his grasp. The other man took a step back and raised his gun but before he could fire a shot rang out from somewhere behind Rogers and the man went backwards into one of the tables, blood pouring from his stomach. Rogers turned, but even as he did so the place erupted into violence. The deputy might as well have tried to stop a hurricane as prevent King's men from carrying side irons. As if at some sort of signal, shooting burst out from various quarters: somebody screamed and a number of people made for the batwings. Rogers took cover behind the overturned table as a fusillade of shots boomed out. From behind the bar the bartender pulled a shotgun and began firing, squeezing hard on both triggers. As gunsmoke filled the air and the crackle of gunfire filled his ears, Rogers made a run for a corner of the bar. Reaching it, he crouched down, expecting a hail of bullets to come his way, but none did. He couldn't work out what was happening until he realized that he wasn't a target because the owlhoots were fighting among themselves. By intervening, he had become the catalyst which had finally broken the uneasy stalemate which had kept the rival factions from one another's throats. That was why the barman was taking an active part, but on which side Rogers couldn't say. He realized, however, that he had to get out of the Blue Bucket somehow. Shots were ricocheting all around and if he wasn't hit directly there was a big chance a stray bullet would find him.

Keeping below the level of the counter, he edged his way around to a stairway that led to the second floor. The last couple of yards he had to make a dash for it. Bullets sang nearby but he made it to the stairwell and ran quickly up the carpeted stairs. He reached the top and moved down a corridor leading from the landing. The uproar below seemed oddly muffled the further he progressed from the stairs. There were several doors and he tried pushing against them but they did not yield to his shoulder. At the end of the corridor there was a window. Pulling open the casement, he leaned out. The window opened on to an alley running alongside the building. He could not tell if the fight in the saloon had spilled out into the street but if it had, it hadn't progressed as far as the alley. Turning his back and putting his leg through the aperture, he lowered himself, holding on to the window ledge until, having reached as far down as he could, he let himself go.

He landed heavily, falling back into the alley and banging his head against the opposite wall. His knee was jarred but after a moment he was able to get to his feet and then hobble to the end of the alley where it joined the main street. Just at that moment the batwings burst open as a man came flying through. In an instant another man had flung himself upon him. The horses tethered outside began to pull at their leashes as men came running and tumbling out of the saloon. A shot rang out from somewhere nearby and a slug thudded into the wooden wall of the building just above Rogers's head. He went down on one knee as another bullet whined past him. This time he had a feeling that he was the target and scanned the street opposite for an indication of who it was firing at him. He could not distinguish anyone through the melee in the street so, deciding on a change of approach, he turned and, still limping, moved down the alley till he reached the opposite end.

He began to move a little more easily, seeking a point at which he might return to the fray. He hadn't gone far when a shot rang out behind him. He felt a searing pain in his shoulder and fell to the ground. Coming behind him he heard the thud of boots and he tried to roll over to meet his attacker. He could not make out who it was but the man was close to him and had his gun raised. There was nothing he could do and he had resigned himself to the fact that his number was up when there came a ringing cry from the direction of the alley. The man stopped in his tracks, turned and fired but an answering report lifted him from his feet and flung him backwards so that he landed almost on top of the deputy. Someone was running towards him and it seemed he was out of the frying pan only to enter the fire when he heard the familiar voice of Kramer.

'Rogers! Are you hurt?'

The deputy looked up into Kramer's face.

'I've been hit in the shoulder,' he said, 'but I'll be OK. Give me a hand up.'

Kramer reached down and helped Rogers to his feet.

'Where did you come from?' Rogers gasped.

There was a hint of a grin on Kramer's face.

'It would have been hard to miss the furore at the Blue Bucket,' he said, 'but I didn't figure you were involved.'

'Looks like King's pack of coyotes finally turned on each other,' Rogers said.

Back in the main street the shooting was continuing.

'Can you move?' Kramer said.

'Sure.'

'We'd better get back. This ain't goin' to end with King's boys tearing hell out of each other. It doesn't matter which side wins, they're gonna turn on the town next.'

'What about the townsfolk?' Rogers said.

'They're ready,' Kramer replied. 'At least, as ready as they're gonna be. Hell, they'd better be.'

'Come on, this way,' Rogers said.

A little further down the street they moved into another narrow alley. As they emerged from it they could see the fracas still going on down the main drag in the lurid lights of the Blue Bucket. They were about to turn in that direction when suddenly they were almost knocked to their knees by a tremendous explosion from the other end of town. Instinctively they put their hands to their ears as a dense column of smoke began to rise into the air.

'What the hell was that?' Rogers gasped.

'I said those varmints wouldn't stop at fightin' among themselves,' Kramer responded. 'Somebody's lettin' off dynamite. Looks like we got real trouble.'

They paused for a moment. Flames were spreading at the far end of Main Street. Kramer suddenly had an intuition.

'King!' he exclaimed.

'King?' Rogers repeated.

'Yeah. The man set fire to his own barn. Seems to me he might have got a taste for destruction.'

'What do we do now?'

Before Kramer could reply there came another enormous explosion which shattered windows nearby and set their ears ringing. The very air seemed to reverberate and smoke ascended in a great mushroom.

'We'd better get down there quick,' Rogers said.

'You're right,' Kramer responded, 'but I'd say we got our hands full right now with this mob.'

Following Kramer's eyes, the deputy looked back towards the Blue Bucket. Whatever had been happening there seemed to have been resolved. Coming down the street was a big bunch of owlhoots. Whether they were making towards the explosions or whether they had seen Kramer and the deputy wasn't entirely clear, but either way they were coming and there could be no doubt that, fuelled with alcohol, hatred and the stimulus of battle, they were hell bent on killing and destruction. In the vanguard was the erstwhile barman carrying his shotgun which he now raised and fired. The buckshot flew high and wide but it was the signal for the others to open fire. A storm of lead engulfed the street as Kramer and the deputy sought cover.

'Hell, I wish I had the Sharps,' Kramer called.

Kramer had stepped back into the alley and Rogers was crouched behind a water tank. Each of them began to fire, taking careful aim in order to make every bullet count. The drunken mob was firing blindly but even so bullets began to sing uncomfortably near. A shot ricocheted from the lead of the tank with a whistling sound and the water was being churned into a miniature maelstrom. Four of the advancing horde went down and a few of the mob sought shelter but most of them just kept coming on. One of Kramer's guns was empty and he started firing with the other. Rogers was jamming shells into the chambers of his Colt. The mob had spread out, making it harder for Kramer and the deputy to make their shots tell. Kramer looked about desperately. There was no way they could halt the progress of the crowd of gunslicks. If anything, they seemed to have augmented their numbers. The situation looked hopeless when suddenly from the depths of shattered shop windows and from the rooftops an outburst of fire broke out, levelled at the owlhoots. A number of them collapsed, blood pouring from gaping wounds. Others turned their attention from Kramer and Rogers and began to fire back at the new enemy. Their response was largely ineffective because they couldn't be sure exactly where their assailants were concealed. A figure showed itself on a roof before taking cover again behind the guttering. Rogers recognized Reynard Armitage.

'It's some of the townsfolk!' he yelled. 'Looks like they've come good. Maybe we got a chance after all.'

Before Kramer could respond there came another deafening blast from the opposite end of town. Smoke was billowing towards them as Kramer began to consider the options. He could stay where he was, maybe find better cover, and fight off the gunslicks. But unless something was done about the dynamiting, there might not be much of the town left to defend. He looked at the mob of gunslicks. There were still plenty of them but their progress had been arrested. Now that the townsmen had entered the fray the contest seemed more even. Although every gun counted, maybe he could leave the deputy and the townsfolk to deal with matters down this end while he tried to do something about what was happening at the other.

'Reckon you can handle things?' he called.

'Yeah! What you got in mind?'

'To try and do somethin' about King!'

He slipped back down the alley, figuring to get to the far end of town through the back streets. The blackness of the night, palliated by the gleaming snow which covered the ground and the fields beyond, was illuminated now by the lurid light of fires which had broken out in the aftermath of the explosions. The crackling of flames came to Kramer's ears and with it the occasional cries of people who had reached the area and were attempting to dowse the fires. Kramer was about to regain the main drag and join them when he reflected that if he was right about King being responsible, and if he was to have any chance of finding him, he might do better to keep to the shadows. Wouldn't King have done likewise? Maybe King wasn't personally involved and had got his men to do the dirty business but somehow Kramer doubted it. In King's current state, fired as Kramer imagined him to be by a personal hatred of the town and its inhabitants, he would very likely want to do the job himself.

Kramer had almost reached the first of the blown-out buildings. Beyond it were the shattered remnants of two others. Vague figures could be seen moving about dowsing the flames. Kramer stopped. If King was about, he wouldn't want to run into anybody. He seemed to have set the dynamite in a certain order, starting with the outermost of the town's buildings.

In which case he could be in the one Kramer was approaching, unless he had set the dynamite to explode on a timer.

Kramer approached the building. It appeared to be a large warehouse or barn, set maybe thirty yards back from the main street. Walking round the side, he saw a gaping black hole which must be the entrance. The doors were open, which was itself suspicious. Silent and elusive as a spectre, Kramer slipped inside. It was very dark and at first his eyes could pick out nothing but they quickly adjusted. Light reflected from the snow spilled through the entrance but Kramer could see nothing. He moved forward, listening intently for the faintest sound. And then he heard it, a slight movement behind him which might almost have been made by a rat scuttling across the floor. But it wasn't a rat because the door of the building suddenly swung to. Kramer turned. Standing by the door was a dark figure holding something in its hand.

'I don't know who you are,' a voice sounded. 'But if you make one move you are going to die.'

'King!' Kramer said.

'Yes, Zebulon King.'

Kramer could see quite well now. King was standing with a stick of dynamite in one hand and a dimly burning taper in the other. King spoke again.

'Whoever you are, you are my witness that the wrath of heaven has descended upon this place of iniquity.'

'The wrath of heaven?' Kramer repeated.

'I am the angel of vengeance, the angel of righteousness. It has been decreed and revealed to me that this town of evildoers shall be wiped from the face of the earth. They are a generation of fornicators but their time of shame has come.'

With a flash of intuition Kramer realized that King had lost his reason. His best chance lay in humouring him.

'You are right,' he replied. 'They have indeed merited the wrath that is about to consume them. That is why I am here. I too have come to wreak vengeance and destruction.'

'You?' King replied after a momentary pause. 'I do not understand. How can that be? I am the one chosen from of old.'

'You have done well. But the evil is so great that one messenger alone cannot deal with its grossness.'

There was a moment of intense silence. Kramer had put the gun back in its holster and now very slowly his hand inched its way towards the handle. He could discern enough to see that King was confused.

'This cannot be,' he spluttered. 'There can be only one instrument of revenge. You are a liar like all the rest of them.'

Suddenly King's hand moved and he lit the touch paper. As Kramer swung the gun up, King hurled the dynamite towards him. Kramer ducked. The dynamite flew over his head. King was already through the door and Kramer hurled himself forward, reaching the door a second before it slammed to. The door struck his shoulder, causing him to drop the pistol, but all he was concerned about was getting away from the barn. Ahead of him he could see the figure of King and then everything was swallowed up in a shattering roar as the dynamite exploded, ripping through the barn and sending a shower of wood and debris high into the air. Kramer was thrown forward but he regained his feet. His head was ringing and his ears hurt but he retained enough presence of mind to seek out King. After a moment he saw the fleeing figure still running hard and now quite a distance ahead of him. He began to stagger forward in pursuit but something hit him on the head and he fell again. When he got up he could see no sign of his target. He was straining his eyes peering into the luminous night, when suddenly they were dazzled by another blinding flash and he dropped to the floor as a shattering boom rent the night. This time it wasn't another building but something away from the town in the darkness of the empty fields. Kramer was confused but as quietness descended once again he realized what it was. King had been right to call him a witness: he had just witnessed the end of King himself who had been blown apart by one of his own sticks of dynamite. Getting to his feet, he started to make his way back towards the alley down which he had come in search of the man who, either accidentally or deliberately, had just destroyed himself. As he approached he could hear the sound of gunfire but it had become more sporadic. His head slowly clearing, he emerged back on to Main Street just as a number of horsemen came galloping by. They were heading away from the direction of the explosions and when they had gone there was an unexpected lull. Kramer glanced around him. There were many bodies lying along the length of the street which was a scene of desolation. Smoke filled the air and from the direction of the explosions he could see people moving about and the hum of voices. He saw two people coming towards him and instinctively reached for his gun which was no longer there. He had forgotten about it in the heat of the action but it wasn't required because the two approaching him were Rogers and Jess Bruford. Jess was laughing and when they came up they both embraced him.

'Fire and brimstone,' Jess said, 'I think we just ran the last of those owlhoots outa town.'

'Thanks to you and the rest of the men,' Rogers said, 'but I wouldn't be countin' my chips just yet. King is not used to losin'. I reckon him and his men could be back before too long.'

Kramer broke into a wild laugh.

'I don't think so,' he said.

The deputy turned to him.

'How do you figure that?'

'Because King ain't around no more. Unless it's in about a million pieces. In fact, I guess you could say he's finally blown it.'

The defenders of the town, most of whom had attended the meeting at the Brufords, were emerging from their places of concealment on the roofs and inside the buildings. Some of them had sustained wounds but mostly they had come through remarkably lightly. Rogers had been right about the gunslicks being divided among themselves. Neither King nor his men had given any thought to meeting with opposition. They had assumed the townsfolk were too scared to do anything and had discounted them. Too late they had learned their error. Quickly Kramer explained what had happened with him and then they made their way to the end of town to help put out the fires that were still burning. People were beginning to emerge and along the street the undertaker's horse and cart began to collect the bodies. Although folks were shaken and exhausted, when they realized that King was dead and the remainder of his gunslicks had departed, a feeling of relief and joy began to reinvigorate them. Snow began to fall, aiding the fire-fighters. Towards midnight some semblance of order had been restored. The townsfolk, bloodied but unbowed, looked at one another with smiling faces and began to embrace. It seemed hardly credible, but it was true: the blight of King was lifted and they were free again.

A few days had elapsed and the town was looking very like its normal self. The exiles had returned from the mountains and now joined the rest of the townsfolk by the stream on the edge of town. The signpost saying *Kingsville* had been removed and another was lying on its side nearby. Kramer, standing with the Brufords, had his arm around Bonny and Miss Tilly Lush was standing in close proximity to Reynard Armitage. There was an air of expectancy which finally found expression in an outburst of cheering as Riff Rogers, now installed as marshal, came into view, his arm in a sling. Arriving at the forefront of the throng, he held up his good arm for quiet.

'Good citizens,' he called, 'I congratulate you all on what you have achieved. By working together, we have rid ourselves of a blight, which for too long has lain on the community, and now we can move forward to a brighter day.'

Pausing, he gave a nod and somebody raised the new signpost, fastening it into a hole which had been prepared to receive it. The gathered people looked at the sign and another cheer rose into the air.

'The town has been restored,' Rogers continued. 'It is back to what it always was and now always will be. No longer Kingsville, but Dirt Crossing.'

The people cheered and someone began firing into the air. Kramer glanced down at Bonny and squeezed her. Old Jess Bruford leaned towards him and with an ecstatic look on his face, shouted above the tumult:

'Dirt Crossing. A fit and proper name for a town.'